"It's too late for that, Cathy."

"You told me that nothing's too late if you want it enough," she said to Jed.

His smile was twisted, but at least it was a smile. And there was a faraway look in his eyes as he replied, "Yes, I did say that, didn't I?"

Cathy held her breath . . . and her words. There was something so special between Jed and herself right now that she didn't want to chance saying anything that might spoil it.

She wished she could latch on to this rare empathy between them. She wished to grasp it and hang on to it. She wanted to go out and look at the stars with Jed, and to let him bring the heavens to her. . . .

Dear Reader,

Welcome to Silhouette **Special Edition** . . . welcome to romance. Each month, Silhouette **Special Edition** publishes six novels with you in mind—stories of love and life, tales that you can identify with—romance with that little ''something special'' added in.

This month is packed full of goodies in celebration of Halloween! Don't miss the continuation of Nora Roberts's magical new series, THE DONOVAN LEGACY. This month we're proud to present *Entranced*—Sebastian Donovan's story. And in November, don't miss the third of this enchanting series—*Charmed*.

October also launches a new series from Sherryl Woods— VOWS. These warm, tender tales will light up the autumn and winter nights with love. Don't miss *Love*—Jason Halloran's story in October, *Honor*—Kevin Halloran's story in November or *Cherish*—Brandon Halloran's story in December.

We're also pleased to introduce new author Sierra Rydell. Her first Silhouette **Special Edition** will be published this month as a PREMIERE title. It's called *On Middle Ground* and is set in Alaska—the author's home state. This month, watch for the debut of a new writer in each of Silhouette Books's four lines: Silhouette **Special Edition**, Silhouette Romance, Silhouette Desire and Silhouette Intimate Moments. Each book will have the special PREMIERE banner on it.

Rounding out this exciting month are books from other favorite writers: Andrea Edwards and Maggi Charles. And meet Patt Bucheister—her first **Special Edition**, *Tilt at Windmills*, debuts this month! Her work has been much celebrated, and we're delighted she's joined us with this wonderful book.

I hope you enjoy this book and all of the stories to come.

Sincerely,

Tara Gavin
Senior Editor
Silhouette Books

MAGGI CHARLES

AS THE MOON RISES

Silhouette®

SPECIAL EDITION®

Published by Silhouette Books New York

America's Publisher of Contemporary Romance

For Chuck, who, like Jed, sees things his way....

SILHOUETTE BOOKS
300 East 42nd St., New York, N.Y. 10017

AS THE MOON RISES

Copyright © 1992 by Koehler Associates, Ltd.

All rights reserved. Except for use in any review, the reproduction or utilization of this work in whole or in part in any form by any electronic, mechanical or other means, now known or hereafter invented, including xerography, photocopying and recording, or in any information storage or retrieval system, is forbidden without the permission of the publisher, Silhouette Books, 300 E. 42nd St., New York, N.Y. 10017

ISBN: 0-373-09771-9

First Silhouette Books printing October 1992

All the characters in this book have no existence outside the imagination of the author and have no relation whatsoever to anyone bearing the same name or names. They are not even distantly inspired by any individual known or unknown to the author, and all incidents are pure invention.

®: Trademark used under license and registered in the United States Patent and Trademark Office and in other countries.

Printed in the U.S.A.

MAGGI CHARLES

wrote her first novel when she was eight and sold her first short story when she was fifteen. Fiction has been her true love ever since. She has written forty-plus romance and mystery novels and many short stories. The former newspaper reporter has also published dozens of articles, many having to do with her favorite avocations, which include travel, music, antiques and gourmet cooking. Maggi was born and raised in New York City. Now, she and her writer husband live in a sprawling old house on Cape Cod. They have two sons and three grandchildren.

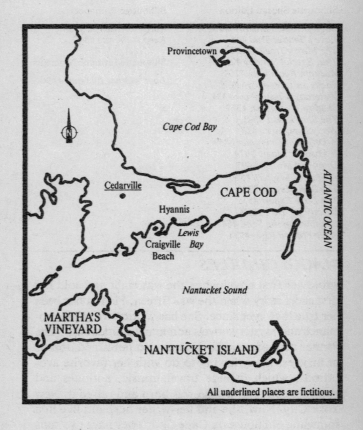

Provincetown

Cape Cod Bay

Cedarville

CAPE COD

Hyannis

Lewis Bay

Craigville
Beach

Nantucket Sound

MARTHA'S
VINEYARD

NANTUCKET ISLAND

ATLANTIC OCEAN

All underlined places are fictitious.

Chapter One

Crows should have squawked. Dogs should have howled. Maybe a meteor should have carved a crater in the parking lot back of the office.

Something should have prepared her for Jed Moriarty.

Cathy Merrill wanted to come up with precisely the right thing to say to him. She toyed with the gold pen her father had given her when she'd graduated from law school. Then she made a couple of meaningless notes on a legal pad as she tried to pull her vocabulary together.

He got ahead of her.

"Nothing personal was intended," he informed her stiffly.

A moment ago he'd reached over and laid a firm hand on the cream-colored file folder with his name on it that centered her desk blotter. He kept his hand in place as he spoke.

Cathy made the mistake of looking up, and their eyes met. His were an intense shade of blue that reminded her of her grandmother's willowware, and were edged with long black lashes.

She had to admit that Jed Moriarty had the most beautiful eyes she'd ever seen. That was the only good thing she could say about him; he was perhaps the most impossible man she'd ever met.

He said, "You mentioned the name of the other attorney in the office...."

Cathy nodded. "Everett Brock."

"Why can't he take my case?"

She reined in her temper. She was not going to let this man see how much he exasperated her.

"Mr. Brock and I agreed to divide Mr. Grant's caseload." She attempted a smile. "You got the luck of the draw, Mr. Moriarty."

He didn't return the smile. Rather, he asked abruptly, "How long will Grant be out?"

A mix of anger, worry and frustration, plus the effects of a sleepless night, eroded a small hole in Cathy's professional facade.

"Bill's still in intensive care," she snapped. "Right now we just hope he'll *live.*"

The scowl she'd begun to think was part of Jed Moriarty's permanent visage was replaced by concern.

"I'm sorry." He sounded as though he meant it. "When you said Grant had been in an accident, I didn't realize it was so serious."

Cathy rubbed her forehead. Her head ached, and being sleep deprived was taking a toll. It was only the middle of the afternoon, and she felt as if this day had been going on forever.

"Bill worked late last night," she said. "It was after ten when he left here. It had been raining. It was foggy. Some jerk coming the other way changed lanes and aimed right for Bill's car. Bill went off the road to avoid a head-on.

"The prognosis is good, but Bill has multiple injuries, including fractures. So, to answer your question, he'll be out of the office for quite a while."

Jed Moriarty finally took his hand off the file folder, and Cathy watched the scowl return. He had an interesting face—high cheekbones, a square chin, a slightly out-of-kilter nose, a wide, well-shaped mouth. A shock of unruly black hair threatened to send an errant curl tumbling over his broad forehead. He was tall—well over six feet, she'd estimated, when she'd looked up a half hour ago to find him filling her doorway.

He was handsome in a rugged sort of way, but he looked about as stern and uncompromising as anyone could, and she deplored his taste in clothing. The dark gray suit was not outstanding, but it was okay. It was his purple-and-red paisley tie warring with his lettuce green shirt that hurt her eyes.

She winced, and reached for his case folder. He immediately shook his head.

"There's no need for you to go into that, Ms. Merrill."

Cathy clutched her gold pen again. "All right," she agreed. "But I *would* like to know why you don't want me to represent you, Mr. Moriarty. If you have doubts about my professional qualifications . . ."

"I don't have any doubts about your professional qualifications."

Cathy forced a sweet smile. "Could it be," she suggested, "that you don't want me to represent you because I'm a woman?"

"No. That's not the problem."

"Then what is?"

Jed looked uncomfortable. "I already told you there's nothing personal involved," he reminded her. "Look, couldn't you switch cases with your associate? What I'm trying to say is, why couldn't you take one of Grant's other cases and let Brock have me?"

Why, indeed?

Everett already had one ulcer. When Cathy had called him shortly after one o'clock this morning to tell him about Bill's accident, she had been left with the feeling that he was on his way to developing a second one.

Since she was technically the attorney in charge of Abernathy, Crowell and DiNatale's Hyannis office, she'd subsequently drawn up a game plan. She'd asked Everett to meet her at eight o'clock. Meantime, she and Gladys Schwartz, the office manager, had arrived on the premises at seven. They'd arranged Bill's files in alphabetical order, then had dealt them out without surveying the contents of the folders.

"One for Everett, one for you, one for Everett, one for you," Gladys mumbled as she doled. "Now, I take it you'll want to see one of your clients, then one of Bill's, then one of yours...."

"You're making my head spin," Cathy complained. "But, yes, that's essentially what I'll do. Meantime, you might call my clients and explain what's happened. Some people will want to reschedule rather than sit around and wait.''

"Will do.'' Gladys nodded.

Everett Brock hadn't been so cooperative.

"Have you called Boston?'' he asked, as he walked into Cathy's office.

"No, it's too early. I'll get around to that later.''

"They'll have to send down another attorney while Bill's out,'' Everett informed her crisply.

"They can't,'' Cathy told him. "At the meeting in the Boston office last week, Mr. Abernathy warned people to stay healthy. They're short-staffed.''

Everett was thin, tense, prematurely gray. For a moment, Cathy wished it were Everett who was going to be out for a while instead of Bill Grant, who was so much easier to get along with.

Forgive me, forgive me. She tried not to look up at the ceiling as she spelled out the silent apology. Then she listened to Everett expostulate about how even Mr. Abernathy—who had deity status in Abernathy, Crowell and DiNatale—would recognize this as an emergency situation.

Cathy had disagreed. "Boston is not about to mount a rescue mission,'' she warned. "Come on, Everett, let's not throw in the towel before we even get started. Once Bill's out of the hospital, we'll be able to call him at home for consultations. That's what he'll want us to do.''

"The added caseload isn't the only issue,'' Everett promptly informed her.

"What is, then?''

"Bill deals with areas of the law you and I do not ordinarily handle.''

"So? We'll have to get used to doing our homework again."

"You're the boss lady." Like his expression, Everett's words were sour.

Cathy had let the remark slide. She *was* the boss lady, and she intended to call the shots.

Cathy looked at Jed Moriarty, and imagined Everett's reaction if she were to turn this particular client over to him.

She said, "Once again, Mr. Brock has all he can deal with right now."

She tapped her gold pen against the legal pad and added, "I have three suggestions for you, Mr. Moriarty. I can arrange to have someone in our Boston office represent you—in which case you'll have to be prepared to travel to Boston for your appointments. Or, you can seek the services of another law firm, and I will be happy to turn your file over to them. Or, if your situation permits it, you can wait for further legal counseling until Bill Grant returns to work."

His answer came fast. "I don't have time to trek to Boston, and my business can't wait until Grant gets back."

"Then suppose I give you the names of some local attorneys?"

"That would be fine with me," Jed Moriarty agreed, then added reluctantly, "provided you'll return the retainer I gave Grant. I paid him fifteen hundred dollars when he took my case. I need that money back if I'm going to do business with someone else."

Cathy told herself she should have known better than to think she could get off this hook so easily.

She said patiently, "You'll have to discuss the matter of the retainer with Bill, once he's well enough. Finances," she explained, "are handled by the Boston office. Bill will need to tell the accounting department how much time he's spent on your case and . . ."

Jed Moriarty's incredibly blue eyes narrowed. "Are you saying my money's gone down the tube?"

Cathy gritted her teeth. "No."

"All right." He leaned back and stretched out long legs that were every bit as muscular as the muscular arms she'd already noted. "I guess," he said grimly, "that we're stuck with each other."

"Oh, no," Cathy retorted, stung. "No, I don't think so, Mr. Moriarty. It wouldn't be fair to either of us for me to take on your case when you feel as you do about having me as an attorney."

Bill Grant's impossible client gave Cathy a slight, rueful smile. "Hell," he confessed, "I don't know how I feel about having anyone as my attorney, under the circumstances."

He shrugged. "Maybe I'm wrong. If so, I'm willing to be corrected. It seems to me another type of lawyer might be more suited to handling my kind of case, that's all."

What had she let herself in for?

Cathy asked carefully, "Just what *is* your kind of case?"

"Bankruptcy. Grant thinks I probably should file Chapter 11."

Jed Moriarty tried to analyze the expression on Catherine Merrill's face as he said that, but he quickly realized she was too professional to give him a clue to her feelings. He doubted she customarily dealt with the seamier side of the law. And—though Bill Grant had insisted he was dead wrong—that's where he put bankruptcy.

"If you'll excuse me," the lady in question said, "I'd like to run through your file."

Jed nodded, and watched her as she scanned the papers in the long legal folder.

She was cool, savvy, beautiful. She had shimmering bronze hair, huge brown eyes, a fantastic figure, and she dressed like a high-fashion model. Jed was sure that with her looks and self-assurance she must come across very well in a courtroom. Regardless, he didn't want to deal with her. She was too beautiful, he thought, too well groomed, too perfect. He couldn't picture her standing at his side as he threw himself upon the mercy of a bankruptcy-court judge.

He wished he could afford to forget about the retainer and get himself another attorney.

He couldn't.

Cathy looked up, then closed the legal folder.

"Mr. Moriarty?"

"Yes."

"You say Bill has advised you to file Chapter 11?"

"He thinks I should take it under serious consideration."

"I'm having a difficult time reading his handwriting. Bill seems to have invented his own shorthand system. He's made a clear note about the retainer you paid him, however."

She met his eyes, and Jed felt as if he were being wrapped in deep brown velvet.

"There's no need for you to worry about the retainer," she told him. "I assure you we'll earn it if you decide to stay with the firm. Otherwise, the major portion of it will be returned to you."

She tapped the folder. "As to your filing Chapter 11... From a preliminary glance at the debt figures Bill has jotted down, it looks as though you'd have to come up with a hefty payment to the court each month if you opt for that kind of bankruptcy."

"If I don't, my creditors will probably close down on me." Jed knew his bitterness was showing.

The beautiful brown eyes zeroed in on him again. They were solicitous. God, was she human after all?

"There may be alternatives," she pointed out. "In order to determine that, I'll need to study Bill's notes further."

Cathy glanced at her desk clock. She'd already spent too much time with Jed Moriarty. She was behind schedule, and the way this day was going, she had no chance of catching up.

She said, "I think that's as far as we can get for now. Gladys Schwartz is our office manager. On your way out, will you ask her to schedule another appointment for you?"

"When can that be?" Jed shot back.

"I'm not sure. Gladys will fit you in as soon as there's an available time slot."

Jed Moriarty stood. He towered over the desk as he said, "I'm anxious to get on with this."

"I realize that."

Cathy made a quick decision. "Since I don't know when I'll be able to see you during regular office hours, suppose we set up an early appointment tomorrow morning?" she offered. "I'll take your file home with me tonight and go over it."

Now why had she taken on overtime work? she asked herself impatiently.

Jed Moriarty said slowly, "I'd appreciate that."

"How about eight o'clock tomorrow morning?"

"Fine."

He straightened the hideous paisley tie, then gave Cathy a charm-laden smile that siphoned the breath right out of her.

"Thanks," he said.

Cathy nodded, but it took a minute before she could get enough control over her voice to speak into the intercom and tell Gladys she was ready for the next client.

The night was a few hours old before Cathy pulled into the driveway of the small house she'd bought shortly after moving to Hyannis two years ago.

There was nothing especially distinctive about the house. She'd bought it because it was on a cul-de-sac that overlooked Lewis Bay, in a secluded older residential neighborhood that was just a couple of minutes from the bustling downtown district.

The apartment over the garage was an extra bonus for which she was profoundly grateful. She didn't need the added income the apartment provided and, initially, hadn't even tried to rent it. Then, several months ago, Gladys Schwartz had mentioned that the place she was living in was being converted into condominiums. She didn't want to buy, and planned to spend the weekend apartment hunting.

Cathy had promptly told Gladys that she had a perfect home for her.

"Right in my backyard," she'd said, then laughed at Gladys's perplexed expression.

It had taken a little persuasion to convince Gladys that it would be a good idea for her to become Cathy's tenant. But by then, a strong bond already had developed between the two women, a rapport that since had strengthened into deep friendship, despite their twenty-year-plus age difference.

Now Cathy wished there were lights on in Gladys's apartment, but the windows were dark.

As she got out of her car, Cathy tried to convince herself that it was just as well Gladys was out. Otherwise, she couldn't have resisted climbing the steps to the apartment, and pouring her list of grievances into an ear she knew would be sympathetic.

This day had been a bummer from beginning to end.

She let herself into a dark house, but before she could switch on a lamp, the ceiling light blazed. Cathy jumped, gooseflesh pricking her skin. Then she heard Gladys's heartwarming laugh.

"Damn," she said explosively, "you scared the hell out of me!"

"That'll teach you not to hand out house keys to tenants."

Gladys crossed the room and gave Cathy an affectionate hug. "Happy birthday eve," she said.

Cathy stared at her. "How did you know?"

"I keep the files in our office, remember?"

"I'm not apt to ever forget again. I knew I should never have hired an ex-school principal to be our office manager."

"Would you have had me wither away from boredom?"

Gladys gently tugged Cathy's shoulders, moving her around so that she faced the coffee table in front of the couch and saw the stack of packages wrapped in bright orange paper.

"You shouldn't have," Cathy immediately protested.

"Of course I should have. Anyway, these are just fun things, but I wanted to give them to you tonight. I thought you'd probably have other plans for tomorrow."

"Given a choice, I'd stay in bed all day with a quilt over my head." Cathy grimaced. "Birthdays are something I'd just as soon forget."

Gladys chuckled. "You haven't exactly reached an advanced age, boss lady. This marks the thirty-seventh, right?"

"Don't rub it in."

"Cathy, thirty-seven isn't even a big one. It's just a step along the way."

"A step in the wrong direction."

Cathy sank down on the couch, her weariness showing. "Today's been such a mess I didn't have time to brood about my birthday, which was fortunate," she said. "When I think about it, all I hear is that old biological clock ticking so loud, it hurts my eardrums."

"Come on."

"It's true, Gladys. Time's rushing by. Another year's gone down the drain, and there aren't many years left."

"Nonsense." Gladys sat down on the opposite end of the couch. "This is a new age we're living in, Cathy," she pointed out. "Many women have first babies when they're into their forties."

"How old were you when you had your first baby, Gladys?"

"This is you we're talking about."

"Yes," Cathy persisted, "but by the time you were my age, you had two kids and—"

"And I was a widow," Gladys finished.

Contrite, Cathy moaned, "God, I'm sorry."

"No need to be sorry. Sherm's been dead twenty years and, as you already know, I like to talk about him. True, he died way before his time." Gladys's eyes misted. "Cancer," she said. "It can be so fast, so deadly."

Cathy bit back a second apology for having raised this subject. Though Gladys *did* frequently speak of her husband, whom she'd adored. They'd both been in college when they married. She'd soon become pregnant, and dropped out. Later, as a widow with two young children, she'd gone back to school, gotten a degree in teaching, then had a successful career in education.

Now her children were grown up, married and had children of their own. Gladys's son lived in Texas, her daughter in California. But from everything she'd heard about them, Cathy had long ago concluded that the Schwartzes were a very united family, despite the geographical distances between them.

She felt a pang of envy.

"Cathy," Gladys said gently, "you look like a child who's standing in front of a toy-store window coveting a doll that's out of reach. Marriage and motherhood are not like that."

"I know," Cathy agreed, her voice soft. "But say what you will, you've had those experiences and you're infinitely richer because of them. Whereas some morning I'm going to wake up and nature will send me the message that I've lost the chance to sing lullabies to my own kids."

She made a face. "Stop me. I'm getting maudlin." She picked up one of the wrapped packages. "Hey, this is all soft and squishy. What is it?"

Gladys held up her hand. "Wait," she commanded. "I have a bottle of champagne chilling in your fridge and I think it's time for a toast."

Cathy watched Gladys walk out of the room, and for at least the thousandth time since meeting her, she blessed the day two years ago when Gladys Schwartz had decided she wasn't cut out for retirement and had gone job hunting.

Gladys was the only person in the world who knew how she felt about getting married and having children. Her peers, both male and female, saw her only as an attractive, successful career person who seemed to be getting exactly what she wanted out of life.

That was far from the truth. For one thing, she'd never wanted to be a lawyer. That had been her father's idea. The judge had been determined to see his only child follow in his legal footsteps, and because she loved him so much, she'd made his fondest wish come true. But at heart she was a frustrated concert pianist.

And her frustrations over marriage and motherhood were infinitely greater.

She knew she'd waited too long to think about her personal future. Through her twenties, she'd been blissfully unaware of the biological clock that ticked so loudly now. Finally it struck her that she wasn't going to many bridal showers for her friends any longer, but mostly baby showers.

Then she'd begun to realize that the men she met either seemed to be married, gay, deeply involved with someone else, or out for an affair and nothing more. . . .

Gladys came back with champagne. She proposed a toast, clinked glasses with Cathy and then Cathy tore the paper off the package she was holding and discovered balloons printed with Happy Birthday, Cathy.

She tried to get into a party spirit of the gesture by blowing up a balloon and aiming it toward Gladys. The air fizzed out of the balloon, and it plopped limply on a couch cushion.

The other presents were all fun things. There was a small black plastic cat with a magnet in his paw that let him stalk and catch a tiny white mouse. There was a box of finger paints with a card on which Gladys had written, "To exorcise your tensions. Just don't show the results to your analyst."

Finally, there was a small brass lamp that looked antique.

Cathy raised an inquiring eyebrow, and Gladys said promptly, "Think of Aladdin. The right magic touch and your genie will grant your dearest wish."

Cathy held the lamp between her hands and smiled a wistful smile. "Do you guarantee that?"

"I would if I could, but you have to tempt fate by yourself. Stroke the lamp and make a wish."

Cathy laughed. "Come on, teacher. I gave up wishes about the time I gave up pigtails."

"Try. Tell the lamp what kind of a man you want, and then wish."

"This is insane," Cathy protested. Nevertheless, she stroked the lamp and crooned, "Genie, if you're in there, let me describe the kind of man I want. The rest is up to you."

She cast a conspiratorial glance at Gladys, then went along with the game.

"I know it's trendy to go for younger men, but I'd like my man to be a few years older than I am. I don't care if he's divorced, but I don't want a widower. I'd hate to have to compete with the memory of a dead wife.

"I definitely go for blond, Anglo-Saxon types. And, Genie, I think the man you find for me should have a profession. He doesn't have to be a lawyer, though I wouldn't mind if he were. I think people have a better chance of staying married if they come from the same background and share the same interests."

"That doesn't sound very romantic," Gladys remonstrated.

"I've been expressing the practical side of my nature," Cathy said. "The romantic side craves someone who is gorgeous and sexy."

"And I suppose this paragon also should be rich?"

"Not rich, necessarily, but financially sound, with good prospects."

"You know," Gladys observed, "I should think you'd have plenty of opportunities to meet a Mr. Perfect through your father."

Cathy smiled. "The judge would agree. He does his damnedest to lure me to Harvard Club dinners and Bar Association banquets. But the men he introduces me to are over sixty, or have already been spoken for."

"Will you be celebrating your birthday with your father?"

"I was supposed to leave work early tomorrow and go up to Cambridge and have dinner with him," Cathy admitted, "but there's no way I can make it."

"Why not?"

"Gladys...you, of all people, should know the answer to that. The office was a zoo today. It's going to be even worse tomorrow."

"Everett could take over if you left early."

"What are you saying? Everett was a wreck by noon, and at that, I spared him from having to deal with one of Bill's clients who would have put him right over the edge."

"Moriarty?"

"Yes."

"He's quite a hunk."

Cathy thought about that. Though Jed Moriarty was not her type, she couldn't deny that he was, indeed, a hunk.

Gladys glanced at her watch. "I think I'd better scoot so we can both get some rest," she decided.

They walked to the door together, and Cathy said, "Gladys...thanks. I may not like birthdays but I liked your surprise party."

"Just keep the lamp handy," Gladys advised. Then, at the door, she turned.

"Cathy," she said, "my maiden name was O'Meara."

"Seems like you've told me that before."

"My family was South Boston Irish. I was brought up strict Catholic. We ate fish on Friday. I still hate fish."

"Why do I have the feeling there's a point to this?"

"Sherm Schwartz came from the Bronx. His family were first-generation German Jews. They spoke Yiddish in his home. Sherm's culture and mine were far apart.

"I guess what I'm trying to say," Gladys went on, "is that love doesn't necessarily come in a box with a lot of diplomas, blue-chip stocks and an impeccable family tree with gold-plated branches. Love is more like a tornado. It can strike anywhere, anytime, without warning.''

Cathy laughed. "I'd welcome the storm."

"Would you?" Gladys asked softly.

Chapter Two

Cathy was frowning as she swung her car into the parking lot back of her office. Her birthday already wasn't going well, and the ordeal of having to call her father and tell him she couldn't make it to Cambridge still lay ahead. She was sure he'd planned an elaborate birthday dinner for her. He always did.

As a starter, this morning her alarm clock had failed her. So much for battery-operated, discount-store imports. She'd had to skip her shower, grab some clothes and bolt out of the house.

She glanced at herself in the rearview mirror. Fortunately she didn't look as frazzled as she felt. That didn't alter the fact that she was almost fifteen minutes late for her appointment with Jed Moriarty, and every minute was precious to her.

Moriarty was waiting for her, sitting in the cab of a red pickup. She saw the slogan Mansions by Moriarty scrolled on the side of the truck, plus a Cape address and phone number.

"Sorry I'm late," she apologized, as she led him to the back door customarily used by staff. "My alarm clock died. I didn't have time for breakfast so I snitched a few seconds to pick up some coffee and Danish on the way over."

He didn't comment.

Cathy noted that he was wearing the same dark gray suit he'd worn yesterday and, again, his choice of tie and shirt was atrocious. The tie featured big red polka dots on a yellow background. The shirt was lavender. Why, she wondered, didn't someone teach him something about mixing colors? A wife, maybe.

She glanced at his left hand. The ring finger was bare. So, maybe he didn't have a wife. But he must have a mother, a sister, a friend. . . .

Her office smelled musty. Cathy raised the shade, opened the window, then transferred a couple of briefs from her desk to a side table, before she faced Moriarty.

"Sit down, won't you?" she suggested politely.

She pushed a Danish wrapped in waxed paper and a cup of coffee across the desk to him, and avoided his disconcerting gaze. She was still rocked by the knowledge that she'd dreamed about him last night. Whether fortunately or unfortunately, she couldn't remember the details of the dream, but a picture of his set, determined face and those blazing blue eyes had been etched into her consciousness.

He pushed aside the cup and said, "Thanks, but I already had coffee."

"Be my guest anyway."

Cathy didn't wait for an answer. She let some of the hot coffee trickle down her throat, then pulled Bill Grant's file folder on Moriarty out of her briefcase.

While she was lining up her gold pen and a legal pad, her nemesis asked, "How's Grant doing?"

"I talked to his wife late last night," Cathy said. "Bill's been having a fair bit of pain, so they're keeping him pretty well sedated. But Beth said the reports are optimistic. It'll be a couple of days before he's up to receiving visitors, though."

She let a small smile escape. "You're not thinking about waiting for further legal counsel until Bill's out of the hospital, are you?" she teased.

The slight attempt at humor misfired. "No," Moriarty assured her gruffly.

Her suspicion that the two of them weren't going to get very far in view of his attitude now resurfaced. She sighed, and confronted the issue.

"Mr. Moriarty," she asked him, "are you sure you wouldn't prefer to contact another firm? I'd be willing to talk with the Boston office and see what I can do about getting your retainer refunded."

He shrugged. "I don't see much point in changing."

It wasn't exactly an endorsement. He might as well have said, "One lawyer's just as bad as another." Cathy fought back a stab of irritation and began, "Mr. Moriarty..."

She decided it was time to get on a more casual footing with him if they were going to work together. "Jed," she amended.

His left eyebrow quirked, and he looked startled.

"I went over your file last night," she said, "but I still had a problem with Bill's system of making notes.

I'll need to work up my own file on you. A lot of what I ask may seem repetitive, but please bear with me.''

She pulled the legal pad toward her, picked up the gold pen. ''Suppose we start with your name?'' she suggested.

The familiar scowl was back in place. ''Jed Moriarty,'' he said.

''Your middle name?''

''I don't have a middle name.''

''Your occupation?''

''I'm a builder.''

''Your address?''

''Cranberry Estates, Cedarville.''

She looked up. ''Is there a street number?''

''No. Cranberry Estates is the name of my development. I live in a trailer on the grounds.''

''Your place of birth?''

''Somerville, Massachusetts,'' he said. And, though she hadn't inquired about his age, he volunteered. ''I was thirty-five last July fourth.''

''Your marital status, Jed?''

She sensed his hesitation. Then he said, ''I'm a widower.''

''Children?''

''No.''

''Are your parents living?''

''No.''

''How long ago did your wife die?''

The scowl deepened. ''What does any of this have to do with filing Chapter 11?'' he demanded.

Cathy wanted to slap back an answer of matching intensity. Instead, she admitted, ''Nothing, probably. I like to draw up a profile on a client primarily for my own information. I feel it gives me a picture that enables me to do a better job of representation.

"Perhaps I should remind you that the lawyer-client relationship is privileged," she went on. "Anything you tell me is strictly confidential—"

Jed held up his right hand. "Hold it," he protested. "You don't have to throw the whole book at me, Cathy. I see where you're coming from—"

"Ah...Jed...how did you know I'm called Cathy?"

"Your key ring has your nickname on it. I noticed it when you opened the door."

"I see." Suddenly her cheeks felt sunburned.

She bent her head over the file folder. "You've given Bill some facts and figures," she said, "but I'll need more."

"That doesn't surprise me," Jed conceded. "Grant said the same thing. I was supposed to have all the information he needed when I came in here yesterday. But the weather's been good and I've been trying to get in as much work as possible."

He gave her a weary smile. "By night I'm usually pretty bushed. But I know you need more figures, and I'll get them to you as soon as I can."

The weary smile turned into a lopsided grin that had an unexpected appeal. Cathy fought a crazy urge to reach across her desk and clutch his hand. She wanted to tell him that regardless of how all this might seem, everything would turn out all right.

Would it?

She said carefully, "You must have run into some pretty heavy problems to be thinking about filing Chapter 11. What happened?"

He shrugged. "A lot of things."

She waited for him to elaborate.

He didn't.

She tried again. "Did you overextend? I know a lot of builders overextended before the economy went sour, then they got caught in some serious binds...."

She saw that he was staring at his hands. They were strong, square, capable hands. She could visualize him working with those hands. She could also imagine that hands like his might sometimes have a very gentle touch....

She curbed her imagination.

Jed said slowly, "I came into some money a couple of years ago, and I had the chance to get some land here on the Cape with development potential for a good price."

He studied his shoes this time. "Mine isn't a large development," he said. "Sixteen one-acre house lots in all. But it's nice land—rolling, centered around a pond that's good for swimming and fishing.

"There's a big outlay involved in starting even a small development. Putting in roads, water, underground utilities. My intention was to get the preliminaries done, then build a spec house. When that sold, I planned to build a second house—"

He stopped, and after a moment Cathy prodded. "Is that what you did?"

"In a way. But what happened is that I chose the Meadowlane Savings and Loan to do business with."

"If you were dealing with Meadowlane, don't be too hard on yourself, Jed," Cathy put in. "Their loan officers were too eager, too aggressive, too avid about doing business. They were too willing to loan larger sums than their clients were in a position to borrow. The lure was very tempting for a lot of people.

"Many have been caught in that particular cauldron now that Meadowlane has bottomed out and the Resolution Trust is acting as conservator."

"Maybe," Jed agreed, "but that doesn't alter my bind. The Resolution Trust wants the money I owe Meadowlane paid back in larger chunks than I can manage.

"Also," Jed added reluctantly, "I had some bad luck that set me back."

"What kind of bad luck?"

"Since the bank was so willing to extend credit, I went ahead and built two spec houses. They were finished early this past summer. I was going to put them up for sale at the peak of the season. But before then, they were torched."

"Torched?"

"Suspected arson, which hasn't been proved, so that's held up payment from the insurance company. Regardless, I started putting up another spec house as soon as I could. I've been doing most of the work myself, to save labor costs. But—" Jed flashed Cathy a wry grin "—let's just say that Lady Luck hasn't been smiling on me. I'm behind with my other creditors, as well as with the Resolution Trust payments. The IRS is on my tail for back taxes. So is the Commonwealth of Massachusetts...."

He finished by saying, "That's why Bill Grant thinks filing Chapter 11 may be the way to go."

"Perhaps it is," Cathy allowed. "But it will do a heavy job on your credit rating. I think we should explore some alternatives."

She tapped her pen against the desk blotter. "Have you talked to your creditors, Jed?"

"Hell, yes. At this point I've given up talking to them."

"That may be the problem."

"What do you mean?"

"If you can communicate in the right way, your creditors may become receptive to the idea of extending your limits a little. Some of them may have been burned themselves by Meadowlane, or another savings and loan. They might be willing to give you a second chance."

Jed shook his head. "I doubt that."

"Well, I would say that it would be worth a try to explore some conversational routes before you take the step of filing bankruptcy. We might even be able to evoke a little sympathy from the IRS and the Commonwealth." Cathy gave him a cocky smile. "It has been done."

Jed heard what she was saying, and sensed a condescension he didn't like.

He watched Cathy look over some of the papers in his file folder. He had to admit she was a smooth talker and she sounded very sure of herself. But she made him wish he could take her down a peg.

She was making notes again on the yellow legal pad. As she leaned over, her breasts strained against the fabric of the white blouse she was wearing. Jed imagined cupping his hands over those breasts, then nuzzling her silky hair, then experimenting with little zones of erotic feeling, nibbling at the small hollows behind her ears and...

What the hell was possessing him?

He had been leaning back, but now he brought the chair legs down with a resounding *whack*. Cathy looked at him, and for an eloquent second their eyes communicated, transmitting silent messages neither of them could control. Then Cathy began to make more notes on the legal pad, her pen traveling rapidly across the pages.

Jed felt the tension between them elongate until it stretched like a length of thin, vibrating wire. It occurred to him that the two of them could get hopelessly entangled.

Cathy kept on writing and talking. "I suggest we meet again the first of the week. That will give you the weekend to get together the material I need. Gladys should be at her desk by now. She'll make an appointment for you."

"All right."

"One thing before you go."

"Yes?"

"How much did Bill Grant tell you about filing Chapter 11?"

"Well, I'd thought declaring bankruptcy meant you lost everything. Grant explained there are different kinds of bankruptcy. He was going to give me some material to read."

"That isn't necessary," Cathy said. "The reading material would be quite technical."

God, but she could be patronizing!

"There are specific sections in the Bankruptcy Relief Reform Act of 1978 that offer help to individuals or businesses ridden by debt," she informed him. "Chapter 11 involves debt reorganization, which is a far less drastic step than filing Chapter 7, which really is a last resort."

Jed jammed his lips together in an attempt to avert an outburst. She was putting him down, whether consciously or subconsciously, and he resented it.

"There are certain qualifications for Chapter 11," Cathy went on. "We need to be sure that you meet them—"

"Frankly, Ms. Merrill, I wish you would give me some material to read."

"I've told you that isn't necessary."

"Why don't you let me decide what's necessary and what isn't."

Jed's tone alerted Cathy. She looked up and saw that his deep blue eyes were sending out angry sparks.

Puzzled, she asked, "Did I say something wrong?"

"It isn't what you said, it's how you said it. I can read."

"Did I suggest you couldn't?"

"You seem to think your legal literature will be way over my head. Maybe you're right, but I'd like to find out for myself."

Cathy carefully laid down her gold pen. Jed Moriarty looked like a boiler working its way up to a full head of steam, and she couldn't see how she merited that kind of behavior.

She deliberately kept her voice low. "I don't know why you should have taken offense to anything I said," she told him. "But evidently you have. If so, I'm sorry."

Jed looked her straight in the eye. "I doubt that," he said.

"What?"

"I doubt you're sorry," he repeated. "You're trying to ease over a rough spot. I appreciate that, but I don't think you understand why I'm irked.

"I may not be a lawyer, but I'm capable of dealing with facts and understanding what I need to understand. You're giving me the impression you think I'm incompetent because I'm in a financial mess."

"Wait a minute," Cathy protested. "I already told you that considering your involvement with Meadowlane Savings, your 'financial mess,' as you term it, is understandable. You're not alone, believe me."

"Regardless. What I'm asking is that you give me a break. Let me attempt to do my own thinking and find out what I need to know."

"Very well." Cathy pressed her lips together tightly for a minute, then said coldly, "Believe me, I'm not trying to keep you from learning anything you want to learn. I can't let you take reference books out of the office, but I'll have Gladys photocopy everything we have in print about the Bankruptcy Act of 1978."

Jed subsided a little. "All I want is some basic information." He smiled faintly. "I don't need a whole law library."

"Nevertheless . . ."

Cathy spoke into the intercom and gave Gladys succinct instructions. Then she said, "That should do it for now. I'd appreciate it if you'd wait in the reception room while Gladys puts together the material for you. I have an appointment with another client."

Jed couldn't take his eyes off her. Though she spoke calmly, she looked flustered. She'd chewed off half her lipstick and run a hand through her hair, momentarily disheveling it. The effect made her tremendously desirable.

He reacted with a swiftness that staggered him. He was still reacting when Cathy spoke again.

"One more thing before you go," she said.

"Yes?" Jed asked hoarsely.

"We may need to meet with some of your creditors. If we do, I'd appreciate it if you'd do something about your attire. You should make the best impression possible."

Jed's eyes narrowed. "Could you spell that out?" he asked, a shade too politely.

"Your shirts and ties don't match."

A mix of emotions roiled in Jed. He glared at her, and couldn't control himself.

"What I wear is my business." The tension that had been building in him found release in anger. "I wouldn't think of criticizing your clothes, and I consider it out of line for you to criticize mine. If you find my shirts and ties offensive, put on some dark glasses."

Jed turned on his heel and stalked out of the office, giving himself the satisfaction of slamming the door behind him.

Gladys poked her head around Cathy's office door toward the middle of the afternoon.

"You didn't even stop for lunch," she accused.

"I didn't have time," Cathy mumbled, as she finished some notes she was making, thrust papers into a file folder and pushed the folder to one side of her cluttered desk.

She was tired, grumpy, resentful. She strung out a series of negative adjectives as she looked up at Gladys. The day had lived up to her worst expectations, starting with her alarm clock's failure this morning and then peaking when Jed Moriarty stormed out of the office.

To make matters worse, thoughts of Moriarty had been distracting her all day, and she couldn't afford to lose her concentration. A clear head was always needed where the law was concerned, and that was particularly true under the present circumstances.

She was beginning to think maybe she should turn him over to Everett after all. If he gave Everett another ulcer, so be it.

Gladys queried gently, "Cathy?"

"Yes?"

"Did you?"

Cathy blinked. "Did I what?"

"Did you make plans for tonight? This is your birthday."

"Gladys, how could I possibly have made any plans for tonight? It'll probably be midnight before I get out of here."

"No, it won't be," Gladys told her. "I took the liberty of postponing some of your appointments until tomorrow so you could catch up. The clients were most cooperative. That means you can walk out of here by six. If you don't, I'll have the electricity turned off and the phones disconnected."

Cathy had to laugh. "I wouldn't put it past you."

"Don't. I know it won't be particularly exciting to spend your birthday evening with a woman old enough to be your mother, but . . ."

Cathy groaned. "Please don't mention birthdays. As it is, I'll have to go up to Cambridge on Sunday and play belated birthday girl to appease my father."

" . . . I want to take you out to dinner tonight," Gladys insisted. "Then, if there's time, we can catch a movie."

Cathy saw the caring and concern on Gladys's face, and was touched. "I'd like that," she said.

"Great. I'll expect you for a glass of wine at my place at seven, all right?"

"Yes, ma'am."

It was a few minutes past six when Cathy's last client departed. She left her desk a mess and bypassed Everett's office, where he was still working.

As she pulled into her driveway, Cathy saw that there were lights on in Gladys's apartment. She glanced at her watch, realized that she had thirty-five minutes to get ready and headed upstairs.

Cathy was just emerging from the shower when she heard someone thumping on the back door. Gladys, she assumed. Possibly with a change of plans.

Cathy pinned her damp hair in a heap on top of her head, slipped on a terry robe and went downstairs. But it wasn't Gladys standing on her threshold. It was Jed Moriarty, looking slightly larger than life.

She gazed up at him, and thought whimsically that if she believed in genies she'd think the one in the Aladdin's lamp Gladys had given her was playing a trick on her. This big, handsome man looking down at her was about as quintessentially male as anyone could be, and she was almost sorry that he was so wrong for her.

She reminded herself of the qualifications for Mr. Perfect she'd listed to Gladys last night. Jed Moriarty was the antithesis of all of them. He was younger than she was, he was a widower, he didn't have a professional background, he was in a financial hole....

He said abruptly, "Sorry to disturb you, but I need to talk to you."

Cathy frowned at him. "How did you find out where I live?" she demanded. "My home phone's unlisted."

"I called your office. Brock was still there. He gave me your address."

She swore under her breath. Dammit, Everett should have known better.

"I'm sorry, but whatever you want to talk about will have to wait," she told Jed stiffly. "I have a dinner engagement and I need to get ready."

"This will only take a minute."

"I don't have a minute." Cathy started to close the door.

Jed stopped her by spanning the side of the frame with his hand. "I don't want to be disagreeable, but I have to get this off my mind," he told her. "So, may I come in?"

"No," Cathy snarled, and then was appalled at herself. She had just violated the ingrained code of good manners by which she lived.

"Jed," she amended, "I really am in a hurry. So, please call the office tomorrow and make an appointment. I'll see to it that Gladys sandwiches you in." She added, "Certainly there's nothing we could do tonight that can't wait until tomorrow."

She fell silent, and a strange, intimate stillness crept between them. Jed's voice broke into it, low and provocative.

"Isn't there?" he asked. He heard himself, and mentally slammed on the brakes. "Okay." He sounded just a shade huskier than usual. "I've already made an appointment for Monday. I guess we can talk then."

"No." Cathy discovered that being unsure of one-self created out-of-character impulses. She capitulated. "Come on in. Five minutes one way or the other won't matter that much."

Jed followed her into the living room. His eyes fell on the coffee table, still strewn with orange paper and Gladys's fun presents. He saw the Happy Birthday balloons, and his dark eyebrows lifted.

"Is this your birthday?" he asked.

So much for leaving evidence in plain sight. "Yes," Cathy admitted.

"Someone's having a birthday party for you, is that it?"

"No. I'm going out to dinner with a friend."

A sheet of orange paper had drifted to the floor. Cathy bent down, picked it up and asked, "What did you want to talk about?"

She turned as she finished the question, and instinctively backed away. The full impact of Jed as he looked right now was . . . overwhelming.

He was wearing a cable-knit cream-colored sweater. His jeans fit snugly over his impressive thighs. His hair looked as though he'd just washed it. It was a mass of unruly curls. He gave her a disarming smile that could have melted an iceberg, and she gulped.

"I'm sorry I came on so strong today," he said. "For my own peace of mind I had to come over and tell you that. You were riling the hell out of me with your attitude."

"I got that message."

"Actually," Jed said, "I was just beginning to calm down when you mentioned my clothes. That put me over the edge."

"I can't blame you." Her smile was remorseful. "You were right. I was rude. I've thought about what I said all day, and I'm so embarrassed, I'd like to go somewhere and hide—"

"No," he cut in, "I'm sure what you said was justified. But I don't really know—because I'm color-blind."

"What?"

"I said I'm color-blind. And . . . well, I guess I'm a little defensive about it. I see colors," he explained. "I just see them my way. Sometimes I'm right, sometimes I'm not. I'm better on some colors than I am on others. Like your hair. It looks like amber to me. I'm right about that, am I not?"

"I . . . suppose so." Cathy was trying not to meet those distracting blue eyes.

"I thought I had on a pale gray shirt today with a red-and-gray polka dot tie, and it seemed to me that would be an okay combination." He paused. "What *did* I have on, Cathy?"

She had to smile. "I don't think you want to know."

"Try me."

She laughed. "No."

"Okay." He grinned. "Tomorrow I'll buy a couple of white shirts and a black tie, and I'll stick with them."

"It might inhibit you to limit your options like that," Cathy teased.

"I'll take that chance."

The grandfather clock in the living room chimed. "I really do have to rush," Cathy said reluctantly.

Jed nodded. "Thanks for letting me get this off my chest."

Cathy looked at his chest, and wanted to pillow her head against it.

She trailed after him to the door. On the threshold, he turned and placed his hands on her shoulders.

"Happy birthday, Cathy," he said, "and may you have many more."

Then he kissed her.

He didn't move his hands. He just kissed her.

He kept the kiss simple. He didn't begin any explorations. But his lips alone communicated in a way that made Cathy feel as if she'd been lit up inside. She melted in Jed's arms as he bathed her in gentleness, tenderness, while at the same time making her intensely aware of a carefully banked fire of potential passion.

She stood on tiptoe, and her arms stole around his neck. She smelled a special scent that blended man, after-shave and outdoors. His hair was soft, springy, and she twirled her fingers through it.

When he released her, she looked up at him, slightly dizzy and very uncertain. Through her private haze, she recognized that Jed Moriarty had a lot of restraint, maybe more than she did. Though she didn't know very much about him, that came across to her. And she suspected he'd learned about exercising self-control the hard way, the way he'd probably learned about most things.

The early October moon was draping silver swatches over Lewis Bay. Jed, silhouetted against the glistening background, said quietly, "Have a great time tonight."

"Thank you," Cathy managed, as she fought the urge to reach out, tug at his arm and bring him back to her. It was a battle she knew would have been lost in an instant had he not walked away from her.

Chapter Three

Judge Merrill opened the door of his condo so quickly that Cathy barely had time to get her hand off the elaborate brass knocker engraved with the large letter *M*.

"How's the world's most beautiful attorney?" he asked.

He bent and kissed Cathy's cheek. "A very happy birthday, my dear."

Cathy preceded him into the large living room, its focal point the picture window that overlooked the Charles River. On the opposite shore, the lights of Boston were beginning to twinkle like captive fireflies.

She accepted a glass of champagne from the judge, and smiled at him. Though he often drove her crazy, she loved him devotedly.

"Special," he said, indicating the champagne, "as you are."

Touched, despite herself, she murmured, "Thanks."

As she sipped the champagne, which was indeed special, Cathy reflected that her father should be in the diplomatic corps. He had an astonishing ability to charm, coerce, influence and inevitably get his own way.

She knew his capabilities only too well. In his low-keyed but relentless manner, he'd kept at her to take up law as a career until he'd won out.

She supposed her success showed he'd been right...to a point. She'd been on the law review as a student, had graduated with top honors, then joined the prestigious Boston firm of Abernathy, Crowell and DiNatale. When the firm decided to open an office in Hyannis, on Cape Cod, she had been offered her present position.

The seventy-odd miles between Hyannis and Cambridge did make a good buffer zone between her father and herself, and most of the time she was grateful for it. Even now, it rankled sometimes to think of how she had given in to the judge over the years, how she'd let him talk her out of her first career choice.

Would she have made it as a concert pianist?

She took another sip of champagne and accepted the fact she'd never know.

"How was the trip up?" the judge asked her.

"Sunday has its pluses. At least there're no real traffic jams early in the day."

"The Cape still seems like a hinterland to me," the judge mused. "Beautiful, yes, but..."

Cathy didn't pick up the gauntlet. She knew exactly where her father was heading.

"Are you keeping busy down there?" he asked her.

She almost smiled. "Yes."

"Catherine," he said with deceptive mildness, "you've been made a junior partner. Now you should be back in the Boston office. You know that."

They'd been this route many times before.

"I enjoy what I'm doing in Hyannis," Cathy reminded him. "There are plenty of challenges, and the pressure isn't so intense. Usually."

He picked up on the "usually."

"Something going on?" he asked.

"I think you met Bill Grant one time when you were visiting me. He was in a bad accident the other night. So Everett Brock and I are shouldering his caseload while he's out."

"Why doesn't the firm send someone down to help you?"

"They're short-staffed just now."

"All the more reason why they need you in Boston," the judge said promptly. And before Cathy could question his logic, he added, "Senior partnerships come to those who are the most visible."

"Dad, I'm not ready for a senior partnership."

As she said that, Cathy thought of Abernathy, Crowell and DiNatale's senior partners. Most of them seemed older than her father, and the judge was sixty-four, though she had to admit he looked younger.

He was a handsome man, with thick white hair and clear gray eyes. He had a good physique, and kept himself in shape working out and swimming at a local health club. He played an expert game of bridge, and had a cabin on a lake in Maine where he retreated when the urge to do some serious fishing arose. Sometimes he invited Cathy to go with him; sometimes she accepted. Sometimes he took along a couple of male legal cohorts.

He was also a surprisingly good dancer. This past spring, he'd wheedled Cathy into going to a Bar Association banquet with him. She couldn't remember when they'd ever danced together before, and she'd been genuinely astonished by the way her father moved around a ballroom floor.

He was a real catch, Cathy thought, but where women were concerned he was elusive. She'd been twelve when her mother died. To her knowledge, her father had never had a relationship with a woman since. He didn't even date.

It occurred to her that she should have done something about stoking up a few fires for the judge a long time ago, and it still wasn't too late to begin. Unfortunately, she was a rotten matchmaker, whether for the judge or herself.

Eduardo appeared with a tray of hors d'oeuvres. Slight, wiry and olive-skinned, with jet hair and black eyes, Eduardo was probably in his early forties by now, Cathy imagined, though he looked younger.

Eduardo had found himself in trouble shortly after arriving in Boston from his native Puerto Rico several years back, and had faced Judge Merrill in Middlesex Court. The problem concerned Eduardo's involvement in a convenience store holdup in which Eduardo actually had been a bystander.

The judge had been sympathetic, and Eduardo had been acquitted. Subsequently, Eduardo applied for the job when the judge needed a housekeeper, and had reigned in the condo ever since. His loyalty to the judge was unswerving, and he was a fantastic cook.

"Muy feliz cumpleaños," he greeted Cathy.

Although Eduardo could now speak English reasonably well, he had learned at some point that Cathy had taken a couple of college courses in Spanish, and he always addressed her in his native tongue. They got along fine, provided he spoke slowly and didn't say too much.

She smiled. *"Gracias."*

The judge refilled the champagne glasses, then brought forth two beribboned packages.

The first contained a bottle of Fracas, Cathy's favorite perfume. The second smaller box held an exquisite diamond-and-opal ring.

There was an unaccustomed sadness to the judge's smile as he listened to Cathy's exclamations. Then he said quietly, "The ring belonged to your mother. I should have given it to you a long time ago.

"As you know, her birthday was also in October, so you share the same birthstone. I wish you could have shared so much more with her. She was a beautiful, wonderful person and she would be so proud of you."

Tears surged, and Cathy wiped at them with a fine linen cocktail napkin as she let the judge slip the ring onto her finger.

The fit was too tight on the ring finger of her right hand, but perfect for the fourth finger of the left. The diamonds blazed, and the opal glowed with red, blue and green inner fire.

They moved on to the dining room, where Eduardo served a delicious dinner, then brought in an elaborately decorated cake as a finale. Cathy didn't count the candles, but their sparsity suggested that

Eduardo had chivalrously understated her age. She was sure he knew exactly how old she was. Not much escaped Eduardo.

Espresso was served in the living room. Then the judge asked, "How about a little Debussy?"

He nodded toward the grand piano he'd given Cathy on her twenty-first birthday. She recalled that the last time she'd played the piano it had been hopelessly out of tune, which had emphasized the sad fact that she was the only person who ever did play it.

Her father, she thought, as she often did, led too solitary a life too much of the time. So, for that matter, did she. She didn't like the idea that she'd become a workaholic, but the description was beginning to fit. For a long time she'd been keeping her social life to a minimum.

Now, Cathy glanced at the piano again, and said ruefully, "I can't, Dad."

Music, much as she loved it, was beyond her right now. She just wasn't in the mood.

"I should start back to the Cape before too long," she said, knowing this was exactly what her father didn't want to hear. "I have to get to the office early tomorrow."

She suddenly wished she'd checked with Gladys to see what time Jed Moriarty's appointment was scheduled.

She fingered the handle of the fragile demitasse she was holding. Damn...she didn't know how she was going to deal with seeing Jed again. She wished he'd never shown up at her house the other night and, especially, that he'd never kissed her.

Jed was her client, and she had always felt strongly that a strict, impersonal line should be maintained between lawyer and client. He had stepped over that line the other night and, even worse, she had let him cross it. Now it was up to her to push their relationship back where it belonged.

She drained the last of the espresso. So what if they'd shared some titillating sexual vibes? Regardless, she'd be an idiot to even think about letting her body rule her head where Jed Moriarty was concerned.

If she were looking for an affair, that would be one thing. But she was not in the market for an affair, she was in the market for marriage, Cathy reminded herself sternly. That was something she needed to concentrate on if she were ever going to hold her own child in her arms. And Jed Moriarty, certainly, was not marriage material. Not for her, anyway.

She frowned, and the judge asked quickly, "A problem?"

"I was just thinking of some of Bill Grant's clients I've inherited." Cathy opted for the plural.

"What about them?"

"Bill deals with areas of the law I've never been involved with."

"Such as?"

"Bankruptcy, for one."

"These days," the judge said, "bankruptcy tends to be pretty much of a legal specialty. Not one I'd personally care to handle."

"I agree. But right now I don't have a choice."

"Is there a specific case that you're bothered about, Cathy?"

Was she bothered by Jed Moriarty?

"Er... I just want to be sure the man I'm thinking about should file Chapter 11."

"That shouldn't be too difficult to ascertain."

"I suppose not."

Cathy rose. "Dad, I do have to get going."

Fortunately one thing the judge always understood was the call of duty, especially when it involved the law.

He escorted her to the parking lot, back of his condo, and she felt a swell of tenderness toward him as she kissed him and thanked him for his gifts.

She was in danger of getting too sentimental, because she never liked to see the bleakness that curtained her father's face when she said goodbye to him. But she was damned if she was going to embark on yet another guilt trip. She knew exactly what the score would be if she ever yielded to the judge's wishes.

Those wishes involved her returning to Boston and moving into his condo. Physically, the condo was more than big enough for both of them. In more important ways, even Buckingham Palace wouldn't be large enough to hold the two of them. They would soon grate on each other's nerves.

What they both required, Cathy thought, as she headed across Boston toward the Southeast Expressway, were significant others in their lives. The judge needed not just a woman, but a wife. Cathy needed not just a man, but a husband who would want children as much as she did.

Moonlight covered the road with a silver sheen that seemed to stretch into infinity. As she drove toward Cape Cod, Cathy pondered what it was that made moonlight so romantic, made the inner yearnings so much stronger, the unrequited longing so much more difficult to bear.

A vision of Jed standing against a backdrop of moonlight tantalized her, and she switched on the car radio, deliberately choosing a news station.

This was not a time to listen to music. Music and moonlight were a dangerous combination, especially when blended with thoughts of Jed Moriarty.

Jed woke up early Monday morning to the sound of rain pelting his trailer roof.

He looked out the window and swore. He'd worked all day yesterday framing a third house. He'd had to quit with darkness last night, even though with just a couple of extra hours he could have accomplished a lot more.

Darkness would be descending earlier and earlier, as fall moved toward winter. And when a rainy day like this one cropped up...

He plugged in the space heater to chase some of the damp chill out of the trailer, and made a pot of coffee. Then he looked ruefully at the stack of papers on the table he used as a makeshift desk.

He'd been too damned tired last night to put together everything he needed to give Cathy. But now, in view of the weather, there was no excuse not to get down to facts and figures.

His appointment with Cathy was at five-thirty that afternoon. Her last appointment of the day, Gladys Schwartz, the office manager, had told him.

Jed showered, dressed, warmed a cranberry muffin in his small microwave and drank a cup of coffee. Then he tried to concentrate on statistics.

He couldn't.

His mind kept roaming. He kept thinking of the mistake he'd made in going over to Cathy's house the other night. He'd *kissed* her, for God's sake. That, in itself, wouldn't have been that much of a big deal, but his reaction had astounded him. He had wanted Cathy so much, his body and his soul had ached for hours after, and still felt bruised. And he'd not been alone in that wanting. He'd seen her eyes; he'd accurately gauged the yearning in her. And knew he had to back off, no matter how much it hurt.

It was a good thing she'd had a dinner date, he thought now. Otherwise it would have been close to impossible to summon the willpower to get himself the hell away from her place.

Jed groaned, pushed away a stack of papers and propped his head between his hands.

God knew he had enough problems. He didn't need a beautiful female complication. And he didn't need to discover—the hard way—that Cathy Merrill was out of his league. He'd known that the moment he looked at her.

How was he going to handle meeting her again this afternoon?

The answer to that was easy, he told himself. He wasn't going to have to handle anything. Cathy, he'd guarantee, would have her act together, and she wouldn't miss a beat. She'd juggle the situation for both of them, and she had the finesse to do it.

Jed forced his attention back to his account books and worked until his head started to ache. He took a break, trekked to a little restaurant in the village where the food was both good and cheap and treated himself to a hot lunch.

The rain was coming down harder than ever by the time he got back to the trailer. He made a fresh pot of coffee, and started in on his records again. Soon the phone began to ring.

Creditor calls—all of them.

By late afternoon, Jed was ready to rip the phone out of the wall. He wished he could make people understand that he was going to pay back every cent he owed, and that no one could rue more than he did the day he'd become involved with the Meadowlane Savings and Loan. He would never forget the lesson he'd learned; acceptance of easy credit could have devastating consequences.

He put on his hooded slicker, then drove the back roads to Hyannis. His pickup truck sloshed into Abernathy, Crowell and DiNatale's parking lot at 5:25.

In the reception room, Gladys Schwartz smiled at him, and said, "Ms. Merrill is still with a client, but she should be free in a few minutes. Is it raining hard as ever?"

"Harder, and there's a pretty gusty wind blowing, too—"

Jed broke off as he looked over Gladys's shoulder and saw Cathy ushering out a client.

The client was an elderly man, and Cathy was speaking to him in a soothing tone, as if she were trying to reassure him about something. But her words trailed off when she saw Jed, and her eyes widened.

Jed saw her mouth tighten, and he got her message. Cathy was as uncomfortable about this meeting as he was.

He was immediately on the defensive. He wanted to tell her there was one thing for sure—she had nothing to worry about. History was not going to repeat itself. Henceforth, he would keep his hands—and his mouth—where they belonged.

Cathy invited, "Come in my office, Jed."

Jed followed her.

He'd put the papers he had for her in a large manila envelope, which he'd tried to keep dry, but it was damp at the edges anyway.

He slid the envelope across Cathy's desk and said, "Sorry. It's kind of soggy."

Cathy nodded without comment, sat down in her swivel chair and picked up the gold pen that always seemed to be at her fingertips. She stared at the manila envelope, but she didn't open it.

Jed wished he could read her mind, then decided it was probably just as well he couldn't.

Cathy finally put down her pen, opened the envelope and tugged out its contents. It was then that Jed saw the sparkling ring on the fourth finger of her left hand.

He felt as though he'd been hit with a rock right in the middle of his stomach. It didn't take much thought to put things together. Cathy had said she was having dinner with a "a friend" on her birthday. Evidently the "friend" was a helluva lot more than a friend, and he'd given her the ring.

She'd gotten herself engaged on her birthday.

Jed tried to convince himself that whatever she did was none of his business. He watched her scan his papers. Then she frowned.

"Jed, you haven't given me much more than I already had."

"I had to straighten out a lot of details," Jed admitted. "I've neglected the paperwork and there was a fair bit to untangle."

"Obviously." Cathy looked across the desk, her brown eyes troubled. "Jed, I need more than this."

He nodded. "I realize that."

"Maybe you should just bring in your account books and everything else you have, and we'll go from there."

"That would take too much of your time," he protested.

"It may be time I need to take if we're going to reach the right decision about your next step." Cathy pushed the papers aside. "I know you've been stressed," she said, "but it does appear you've gotten awfully far behind in your bookkeeping."

"Yes, I know, and I'm sorry." Jed found it difficult to think clearly with Cathy's gorgeous topaz eyes zeroing in on him so intensely.

"Hey, there's nothing to be sorry about." For a minute, Cathy sounded as warm and human as she'd been when she was in his arms the other night. But some coolness crept into her voice as she added, "You're the one who is in such a hurry to take action. I'm trying to get us to the point where we can manage to do that. So—what's the real problem?"

Jed said uncomfortably, "I guess I need a good accountant. I had an accountant, and I fired him. I needed information, and I couldn't get it from him. Turned out he hadn't gotten around to working on my stuff because I owed him his latest bill."

He added quickly, "I don't mean to imply that I can't handle the books myself. I can. I've had some setbacks. When we have good weather, I've been putting all the time I can into building. Occasionally I hire a part-time helper. But mostly I've been working alone, so the going is slow."

Jed wished Cathy wouldn't look at him so steadily. He moistened his lips, and went on. "I'll have to get into subcontracting before much longer—plumbers, electricians. Fortunately I have guys who are still willing to work for me because they know I'll pay them as soon as I possibly can. Maybe I can put in more time on the books when they're working."

He lifted his shoulders, as if trying to rid himself of heavy weights. "Even on a day like today, when I *can* hole in and work on the records, there are endless interruptions," he allowed.

"Interruptions?"

"Creditor calls," Jed said. "I don't blame the guys who make them—it's their job. But with the phone ringing off the hook, it's hard to get much done."

Cathy's nod was curt, because she was trying to rein in her emotions. The grin Jed was giving her was slightly skewed, and she was fighting a ridiculous impulse to kiss it and make it straight.

The intercom on her desk buzzed. Glad of the interruption, Cathy pressed the button. "What is it, Gladys?"

"There's a Frank Winslow on the phone, calling from Washington. I know you said you didn't want to be disturbed, but he insists it's urgent that he speaks with you."

"Did you say Frank *Winslow?*"

"Yes. Do you know him?"

Did she know him? "We went to law school together," Cathy said. As, indeed, they had. Frank was the kind of blond, Anglo-Saxon type that had always appealed to her. He came from a wealthy family; they'd had a lot in common. She'd fallen in love with him—more's the pity. They'd had a relationship, then right after graduation Frank had married a girl from his hometown.

She'd heard via mutual friends that the marriage hadn't worked out; evidently there had been a divorce. She'd also heard that Frank was now an attorney with the Justice Department and lived in Washington.

She suggested, "Ask him if I can call him back, will you, Gladys?"

"He says he's calling from Dulles and he's about to get on a flight to Boston. He wants to set up a meeting with you."

"All right, I'll talk to him."

Jed's ears went on red alert as Cathy picked up the phone, though he attempted to convince himself he wasn't trying to listen.

There wasn't much to make of the one-sided conversation, anyway. Cathy spoke in short sentences.

He heard her say, "Why don't you call me once you're settled in at your hotel, Frank? I'll be home this evening."

His glance fell to the sparkling ring on her engagement finger, and he was perplexed. She seemed to be receptive to the idea of seeing this former law school classmate while he was in New England, yet she'd evidently just gotten herself engaged.

Perhaps he was hopelessly old-fashioned, Jed conceded. But if *he* were Cathy's fiancé, there was no way he could be broad-minded about her seeing another man.

Cathy hung up the receiver and said, "I think I've solved our problem, Jed."

"Pardon?" Jed's thoughts had strayed way off.

"Bill won't be using his office for a while. Judging from the forecast I heard on the car radio this morning, we're in for a fairly long rainy spell. That will keep you from doing much building. So..."

What was she leading up to?

"Bring all your records, papers, whatever, over, the first thing in the morning," Cathy told him. "You can hole up in Bill's office and work without interruption." She smiled. "I guarantee you won't get a single phone call."

Jed stared at her, appalled. This had to be the worst idea she possibly could have come up with. Though he sometimes thought he had more than his share of self-control, the idea of sharing the same space with Cathy was tempting fate to a ridiculous extent.

"I don't think that would work out," Jed said.

"Why not?" Cathy asked innocently. "I'll try to reserve a little time now and then between clients so I can help you out if you run into snags. If you concentrate on this, you should have everything straightened out by the time the weather clears."

Cathy saw his uncertainty, and suddenly felt even more uncertain himself. Those eyes of his were incredible. She'd never seen a more glorious color....

"Come to think of it," Jed said suddenly, "perhaps you're right."

"What?"

"The sooner I can get you the information you need, the sooner we can get on with all of this and get it done," he told her.

It seemed to her that he might as well have added, "the sooner the better," and she fought back resentment. Though . . . he was right, of course.

The sooner they got the work between them over with, the better—for both their sakes.

Chapter Four

Cathy glanced blankly at the aristocratic-looking white-haired woman sitting across the desk from her. "What was that, Mrs. Smithson?" she asked politely.

"I was telling you that I want to be certain Sylvester inherits my entire estate," Genevieve Smithson said rather stiffly. "This new will must be foolproof."

"Yes." Cathy hesitated. "What did you say Sylvester's last name is?"

"Smithson. Sylvester Smithson. At least I think that would be his legal name." It was Mrs. Smithson's turn to hesitate. "Ms. Merrill, have you forgotten that Sylvester is my dog?"

God help her, she *had* forgotten—after reminding herself earlier that she must present a strong argument to convince this wealthy woman of the folly of leaving her fortune to her pet, no matter how beloved he might be.

Mrs. Smithson's pale gray eyes swept over Cathy's face. Then she asked, "Is there something wrong, Ms. Merrill?"

Cathy stifled a laugh that easily could develop into hysteria. What was wrong was that Jed Moriarty was just one wall away from her, and she couldn't concentrate.

She'd awakened at dawn, and immediately begun to berate herself for having suggested that Jed use Bill Grant's office. Even Gladys had raised an interrogative eyebrow when she'd been told about their temporary tenant.

Everett looked bitter as gall when he confronted her within minutes of her arrival in the office, and for once Cathy couldn't blame him.

"There is a person named Moriarty who seems to be making himself very much at home in Grant's office," Everett had reported, his thin face stiff with disapproval. "He referred me to you. Since you were not here, I spoke to Gladys, and she tells me you sanctioned this."

"That's correct." Cathy tried to pretend that she was in court, and Everett was an opposing attorney. "Mr. Moriarty is a client of Bill's. We need him to work up some information for us."

Everett murmured something short and explicit, the mutter so soft, Cathy couldn't be sure she'd heard him correctly. In fact, she felt her ears had to have been wrong. Everett Brock didn't say things like that.

Now Mrs. Smithson said, "His AKA registered name is Sylvester Kensington Smithson."

That did it. Cathy got down to business, and started to outline to Mrs. Smithson some of the reasons why she shouldn't make Sylvester her heir. But before she'd finished with her first point, there was an interruption.

"Cathy?"

Jed Moriarty stood in the doorway, looking fabulous in charcoal slacks and a white turtleneck.

"Excuse me," he said, "but I wonder if you have a spare pocket calculator? I forgot mine."

Cathy heard a slight gasp, and glanced at Mrs. Smithson. She knew her client would be eighty on her next birthday, yet there was a definite spark in Mrs. Smithson's eyes as she looked at Jed.

Cathy remembered her manners. "Mrs. Smithson, this is Mr. Moriarty."

Jed favored Cathy's client with one of his heart-stopping smiles. Cathy, entranced, watched a lovely shade of light rose wash Mrs. Smithson's usually pale cheeks as Jed shook her hand.

She marveled at the effect of the Moriarty charm on someone else. When he wanted to, Jed had so much charisma, it was a shame it couldn't be bottled and sold. But the problem, and also part of the magic, was that he seemed so completely unaware of it.

She reached into her top desk drawer and produced a pocket calculator, which she handed to Jed.

"Thanks," he said, taking it, but Cathy saw that his astonishing blue eyes looked troubled once they turned in her direction. "Sorry I interrupted," he told her. "I didn't stop to think you'd have a client with you. I should have."

"That's all right."

Jed paused to say, "Nice to meet you, Mrs. Smithson." Then he took off.

"Well," Mrs. Smithson said, the pale pink color in her cheeks holding nicely, "I must say he's the best-looking lawyer I've ever seen."

"He's not a lawyer," Cathy blurted, then wished she'd held her tongue. She didn't want to make explanations about Jed, but a glance at Mrs. Smithson told her there was no other way to go.

"My associate, Bill Grant, was seriously injured in an accident the other night, and he'll be out of the office for a while." Cathy hoped to keep this as brief as possible. "Mr. Moriarty is really Bill's client. Just now, he's using Bill's office temporarily."

"What does he usually do?" Mrs. Smithson asked.

"He's a builder."

"Here on the Cape?"

"Yes. He's working on a development over in Cedarville."

Cathy picked up her gold pen. "Now, Mrs. Smithson," she began again, "I understand your attachment to Sylvester, and I'm sure he's a wonderful dog. But I think you should seriously consider some alternatives to leaving your entire estate to him.

"I don't want to alarm you," Cathy went on, "but we have to face the fact that the life span of a dog is even more limited than the life span of a human. Sylvester must be devoted to you, and often a pet mourns an owner to the point where the pet can't...go on. Were Sylvester to outlive you, and that were to happen, the important question is—who would inherit from Sylvester?"

Mrs. Smithson listened, but departed fifteen minutes later without either changing her mind or reaching any definite conclusions.

And the morning marched along.

Shortly after one, Gladys appeared in Cathy's office to say, "Didn't anyone ever tell you that people are supposed to take lunch breaks, boss lady?"

"Gladys, you should have gone ahead to lunch," Cathy protested. "I intended to work right through, but..."

"I wasn't planning a major lunch hour, either," Gladys confessed. "But I persuaded Jed to go over to the deli, and there's some great food spread out on Bill's desk."

Gladys's smile was mischievous. "Thanks to my clever machinations, you don't have another client for almost forty-five minutes, and Everett's gone over to superior court in Barnstable. So, come and enjoy."

The invitation was too good to resist.

Cathy wouldn't have believed that she could curl up in an armchair in Bill's office and relax as she munched, but she did exactly that. And Gladys had both Jed and her laughing till it hurt as she told them about her education in deli food and good Jewish cooking, courtesy of her late husband's family.

The lunch break flew by much too fast. Finally Gladys glanced at her watch, and said, "Take another ten minutes on me, Cathy. You look like you need it. I'll regale the next client with scintillating conversation."

Cathy wasn't in a mood to argue. But after Gladys left the office she murmured, "Do I really look that bad?"

Jed said seriously, "You look terrific. But you do seem bushed. Did you have a late night?"

Jed's eyes, Cathy saw, seemed to be fixated on her mother's ring. Puzzled, she asked, "What makes you think I had a late night?"

"I thought you were going out with your old law school classmate."

What big ears he had!

"Frank is in Boston, not here on the Cape," she said. "He called last night, but there's no way we can get together. He's only going to be in New England for a couple of days. But he'll be back."

She frowned. "How did Frank Winslow get into this?" She turned the frown on Jed. "The reason I seem bushed," she snapped, "is because I've been working too damned hard."

"I couldn't agree more," Jed informed her. "Do you always work this hard, or is it just because Bill Grant's not here?"

"One way or another," Cathy admitted, "I guess I always work this hard."

"Why?"

She stared at him. "Why?"

"Yeah, that's what I asked you. Believe me, I understand the driving urge to work. I suffer from the same affliction myself. But I can tell you from long experience that working yourself into the ground doesn't pay off."

He drew a deep breath. "What about the guy you're engaged to? Doesn't he wish you had a little more time to give him?"

Cathy's frown deepened. "What are you talking about?"

Jed nodded at her hand. "The ring. I assumed you got engaged on your birthday."

She glanced at the fiery opal and the sparkling diamonds. "Well, assume away," she told Jed. "This ring was a birthday gift, yes, but it was given to me by my father. It belonged to my mother."

She stood up. "Now, if you'll excuse me, I'll get back to work."

She didn't slam the door, but she shut it hard. Jed sat back in Bill Grant's chair, and let a long, soft, slow whistle.

There was a knock on the door, and Gladys appeared.

"What happened in here?" she asked, plainly curious. "I just got a glimpse of Cathy and she looked like a thundercloud."

"My fault," Jed admitted. "I thought that ring she's wearing was an engagement ring, and that seemed to annoy her."

"Mmm," Gladys said.

She sat down in the chair Cathy recently had vacated, and said honestly, "To tell you the truth, Jed, I wish that *were* an engagement ring on Cathy's finger."

"Why?"

"Cathy *should* be engaged, she should get married, she should have kids. That's what she wants out of life."

Jed's smile was skeptical. "Are we talking about the same woman?"

"Indeed we are."

"Come on, Gladys. If Cathy Merrill wanted to get married and have kids, she'd do it."

"It takes two," Gladys pointed out.

"Yeah, and I imagine the candidates must be lined up from here to Boston."

Jed sounded morose, which Gladys found interesting.

"Actually," she said, "Cathy can be intimidating to men. She's beautiful, brilliant, highly successful, and while she isn't rich-rich, she inherited money from both her mother and her grandmother that she's never had to touch.

"That," Gladys continued carefully, "might bring out some fortune hunters, I suppose. But Cathy is extremely quick to spot a phony."

"Yeah, I'm sure she is. But—" Jed looked gloomy "—there must be a whole parade of guys who wouldn't give a damn whether Cathy had a cent, or was a lawyer, or—whatever. I admit she can be intimidating. But there's a lot behind that—"

Jed broke off, and Gladys surveyed him with added interest. She'd met Jed Moriarty when he had his first appointment with Bill Grant, and had thought he looked like quite a guy. The more she saw of him, the more she liked him.

True, she would never mentally have paired him with Cathy. There couldn't be two more different people in the world. But . . .

Gladys thought of Sherm.

Cathy, in her office, was trying very hard *not* to think of Jed. She didn't know why clarifying the issue of her mother's ring had bothered her. Had she been subconsciously wishing that she *was* wearing an engagement ring? she asked herself. Was that why she hadn't as yet taken the ring to a jeweler to be sized so she could wear it on her right hand?

She plunged into work with a vengeance. She still felt irritable, however, and when the phone rang a little later she picked it up and growled, "Yes?"

"Hello, beautiful barrister," she heard Bill Grant say.

"Bill," Cathy squealed, delighted. "You're talking!"

"That part of my anatomy is relatively unimpaired." Bill's voice sounded weak but firm. "The rest of me is something else again."

"You must hurt like hell!"

"I did, but it's not so bad now. Or maybe I'm just getting used to being stalwart."

Cathy heaved a sigh. "You don't know how wonderful it is to hear you."

"Terrible what a man has to go through to be appreciated." Bill chuckled. "Beth tells me you and Gladys devised a kind of lottery system to divide my clients up, and you drew Moriarty."

"Yes," Cathy murmured cautiously.

"How are the two of you getting along?"

"I'd say our relationship is akin to a roller-coaster ride."

"Well," Bill said, "I have to admit I've gotten more kicks out of picturing the two of you working together than I have out of most of what I've seen on TV."

He sobered. "Cathy, I know you don't usually deal with Moriarty's type of case, but I'm glad it was you who got him, instead of Everett."

"Jed wasn't," Cathy said ruefully. "Not at first, anyway. He seems to be accepting me a bit better now."

Bill said confidentially, "Jed is the one client who's stuck in my mind, since I've been able to think about anything. Despite that front he sometimes puts up, he's a terrific guy. I wish I could help him solve his problems without filing Chapter 11. I know he doesn't want to do that. Before I got clobbered, I was trying to work out some alternatives. . . ."

"I've been doing my homework, Bill. I'm trying to work out alternatives, too."

"I was sure you would." There was a pause, then Bill said, "Nothing's ever been easy for Moriarty, Cathy. He had a rough time growing up, then he went through a miserable marriage. Finally his wife ran off with another man. She and her lover were killed on their way to Mexico to get divorces. I think maybe that soured Jed on women, so if he hasn't come on to you enthusiastically, that may be why.

"I don't feel I'm violating confidentiality in telling you any of this, since he's your client now. Anyway, I had to dig for my information about Jed. He doesn't readily talk about himself. But I think you need to know as much as you can about him so you'll be able to understand what makes him tick. Otherwise you can't do your best for him. Also. . ."

Cathy waited, then prodded, "Yes?" when Bill didn't go on.

"Cathy. . ." Bill sounded disturbed. "I think someone really has it in for Jed. What I'm saying is, I think he has a serious enemy out there somewhere. He told you about the two spec houses that were torched last summer?"

"Yes."

"There have been instances of vandalism and theft around the development, too. What I would call consistent harassment. I've tried to convince Jed of the strong possibility that there's a definite motive aimed toward harming him behind all of this. He hasn't bought that theory.

"He does admit the fire might have been arson, but he thinks if that's the case, it was the work of a psychopath, not someone with a personal reason to hurt him.

"I hope he's right. I'm afraid he's wrong."

Fear pierced Cathy as Bill talked. Now she asked, "Did you ever talk to the police over in Cedarville, Bill? Or anyone?"

"I've spoken a couple of times with Don Crandon, a private investigator who works on insurance cases," Bill said. "He's working with Jed's insurance company. They still won't pay out, because of the possibility of arson—in which case Jed could have been the perpetrator."

Cathy's denial was quick. "I don't believe that."

"Neither do I. But cases of suspected arson have zoomed the past few years, and arson is very hard to prove. Crandon tells me that in a large percentage of the cases he handles it's almost a sure thing that the fires were set by the owners of businesses or properties trying to get out of financial holes.

"Hell," Bill muttered, "here comes a nurse with a nice big needle. I'll have to ring off."

Before he could hang up, Cathy said, "Wait. Bill, when can you have visitors?"

"As of today, I'm happy to say."

"Then I'll be over to see you as soon as possible. I won't wear you out, but I would like to talk to you a little bit about Jed Moriarty."

"Sweetheart," Bill promised, "you won't wear me out. That's exactly the kind of medicine the doctors haven't ordered for me. They may not know it, but it's precisely what I need."

Cathy slowly hung up and sat back, trying to digest the things Bill had told her. Jed's wife had left him for another man, then had been killed on her way to get a divorce.

No wonder Jed had hesitated over that word *widower* when she'd set up her own file on him. Probably he'd never really felt like a widower. And, but for a twist of fate, he wouldn't have been one.

Cathy had finished with the last client of the day and was stacking some files together when Jed leaned around her half-open door and asked, "May I come in for a minute?"

"Yes, of course," she told him.

"I won't keep you," Jed promised, as he advanced into the room.

"You're not keeping me." She nodded toward a chair. "Sit down."

Jed looked startled, for which she couldn't blame him. She knew he was never sure of just what kind of a reception he was going to get from her—but that worked both ways.

As he sat down, he said, "Cathy, I want to apologize again for barging in on you this morning."

The truth was that sitting there in Grant's office he'd suddenly felt he *had* to see Cathy and so he'd yielded to a crazy impulse, just as he had later when he'd asked her about the ring.

Cathy pushed some papers into a drawer, then leaned back. "Apology accepted," she said.

Her smile was weary. "This has been a long day," she admitted, "but one good thing happened. Bill called."

"How is he?"

"Well, he implies that he's a physical disaster, but he sounds great. He can have visitors now, and I plan to stop and see him on my way home."

"Give him my best, will you?"

"Yes." Cathy knew if she had any sense, she wouldn't get into anything personal with Jed, but she couldn't resist saying, "Bill wondered how you and I are getting on together."

A dark eyebrow quirked upward. "What did you tell him?"

"Well—" she couldn't chase her smile away "—I told him that you were pretty skeptical at first about my taking your case. But that now we're...doing better."

She had to look at him as she said that...and she wondered how his wife ever could have walked out on him. The woman must have been a fool!

He asked softly, "Are we doing better, Cathy?"

"I...think so." She saw the doubt in his eyes and asked, "Don't you?"

"I'm not sure," he admitted. "Sometimes I still get the idea you wish you'd never become involved with my case. Hell, I can't blame you. I—"

She cut in. "I want to do anything I can to help you, Jed."

He looked uncomfortable. "I don't much like the sound of that."

"Why?"

"I'm not asking for charity."

Cathy saw the stubborn thrust of his chin, and groaned. "Simmer down, will you, Moriarty," she suggested. "Don't read things I don't mean into everything I say."

Jed burst out laughing, and after the initial shock began to wear off, Cathy thought she'd never heard anything that sounded better. His eyes sparkled as he said, "Sometimes you and I both have a tendency to misread each other."

"I'll plead guilty to that."

Jed's gaze lingered on her face. She liked the effect, provocative though it was. And she wished she could read Jed's mind, determine just what he was seeing when he was seeing her, just what he was thinking when he thought about her.

How did she come across to him? It suddenly became very important to know.

Cathy's throat felt as though she'd spent a spell without water in the desert. She had to edge into a safe subject, so she asked, "How did you make out with the books today?"

He lifted his shoulders, then dropped them again. "Okay, I guess. It's time-consuming work. I didn't get as far as I wanted to, but there's a limit to how long I can pore over records.

"I'm used to doing a fair bit of physical work. It's hard for me to be cooped up for hours at a stretch." He smiled faintly. "I guess I'd never make a lawyer."

Cathy laughed. "You could have fooled Mrs. Smithson."

"What do you mean?"

The words were halfway out before she could retract them. "She thought you were the most handsome lawyer she'd ever seen."

Jed, impassive, muttered, "She must need her glasses changed."

"I don't think so."

Except for a quick blink, Jed's expression didn't change. Then he deliberately altered the course of the subject. "Did you always want to be a lawyer?" he asked.

Cathy shifted mental gears and admitted honestly, "No. My father wanted me to be a lawyer."

"You gave in to him?"

"It wasn't really that simple. I guess maybe I didn't have enough confidence in myself to do what I really wanted to do." She'd never put it quite that way before, even to herself.

"Also... I did want to please my father. He was in practice for many years in Boston before he became a Middlesex County judge—which is what he still is. I was his only child. My mother died when I was twelve. After that, I think my father's sole aim in life was to have me follow in his footsteps. He knew, of course, that he was never going to have a son."

"What did you really want to do, Cathy?"

"I wanted to be a concert pianist."

Jed, surprised, said, "I didn't see a piano in your place."

"I don't have one. The judge gave me a grand when I was twenty-one. It sits in his condo up in Cambridge, and the other night when he asked me to play something for him, I couldn't bring myself to do it. I knew the piano would be so out of tune, it would hurt my ears, and my fingers would work the keys as if I had boxing gloves on."

"Sounds like you still love music."

"I'll always love music."

"I mean, you sound as if you'd still like to play."

"Too late," Cathy said.

"Nothing is too late if you want it enough."

Some things are, she wanted to tell him. *Sometimes it's too late for a woman to have a child.*

"What about you?" She switched the tables on him.

"What about me?"

"Did you always want to be a builder?"

"Hell, no. I wanted to be an astronomer."

He smiled at her expression.

"I told you I was brought up in Somerville," he said. "Like most places, Somerville has some good neighborhoods and some very bad ones. We lived in one of the very bad ones. We lived in a dump, in fact, until I was fourteen. That's when my father was killed."

His voice lowered. "The only good thing about where I lived was the night sky," he said. "That was fantastic. I used to sneak out of bed and go out to the alley between the three-decker we lived in and the one next to it, and I'd lean against a bulkhead and stare at the sky.

"Sometimes my father would come home and catch me out there. Then he'd take the back of his hand to me."

Jed didn't add that on those occasions his father was almost always rip-roaring drunk.

"I got a paper route when I was about eight. I had to turn most of the money I made over to my father, but I saved up some of my tips until I had enough to buy a book on astronomy that had charts in it. I figured out a lot of the constellations, and I got to know one planet from another. Even when it was so cold I damn near froze, I sneaked out whenever I could and studied the stars and memorized what I was seeing. Then, later, I'd look up what I'd seen so I got to know the Pleiades, and Orion, and Cassiopeia. I found out that what looked like a fuzzy star at the top of Perseus was actually the Great Cluster, and the star at the bend in the Big Dipper's handle is called the 'Horse,' and right above it is the 'Rider.' Long ago, Arabs had another name for the 'Rider.' They called it the 'Test.' They said if you could see it with the naked eye it proved you had good eyesight. I could see it."

"Didn't you ever have field glasses, or even a small telescope?"

"Are you kidding?"

"Jed, it still isn't too late for you to study astronomy. And once things have straightened out, you can get yourself a telescope. Even a small one, as a starter, would open up the heavens for you."

Cathy discovered it was important to her that she convince him he could do this.

Jed shook his head. "It's too late for that, Cathy."

"You told me that nothing's too late if you want it enough."

His smile was twisted, but at least it was a smile. And there was a faraway look in his eyes as he said, "Yes. I did say that, didn't I?"

Cathy held her breath . . . and her words. There was something so special between Jed and herself right now that she didn't want to chance saying anything that might spoil it.

She wished she could grasp and hang on to this rare empathy between them. She wanted to go out and look at the stars with Jed, and to let him bring the heavens to her. She wanted to play the piano for him as she used to play it, her fingers mastering the ivory keys so that she could take him into her world of music.

She thought suddenly of the little Aladdin's lamp on her coffee table, and she silently asked, Genie, what have you done to me?

Maybe when she got home tonight she'd better rub the lamp again, and make a safer wish.

Chapter Five

Cathy, shocked by her first glimpse of Bill in traction, tried to make light of her reaction. She kidded, "You look like a strung-up marionette."

He chuckled. "Thanks for telling the truth. When my mother came in to see me, she burst into tears. Then she said, 'Bill, you look wonderful.'"

"You look wonderful to me, too."

"Remind me to send you roses when I get out of here." Bill attempted to switch position without much success. Cathy grimaced sympathetically. The hospital personnel did have him firmly anchored.

"Beth's gone down to the cafeteria to get something to eat," he told Cathy. "I wish I could get her to leave this place for a while. She's become a fixture."

"This is where she wants to be, Bill."

"Yeah, I know. And I know I'm lucky."

Bill gave Cathy the kind of careful scrutiny he was very good at, then said frankly, "You look beat, boss lady. Hell, I'm sorry. The added workload I've laid on you is unfair."

"You didn't exactly choose this kind of vacation, comrade."

"Even so."

"Jed said to give you his best," Cathy added, remembering Jed's request.

"Tell him to get himself over here. For once, we can skip talking about legal problems and get into fishing and some of our other common interests." Bill favored Cathy with a wicked grin. "Women, maybe."

"Beth should hear you."

"Believe me, Beth knows she has nothing to worry about."

Bill was tall, blond, attractive, but Cathy was sure that Beth Grant really didn't have anything to worry about where her husband's faithfulness was concerned.

Cathy's pang of envy was unavoidable.

She turned her thoughts to something Bill had just mentioned. Curious, she asked, "Did you say you want to talk to Jed about *fishing?*"

Bill nodded. "I promised I'd give him casting lessons. I guess I won't be able to keep the promise this year, but by the time the stripers are running next spring, I'll have him out on an ocean beach, if I have anything to do with it. The one thing he's bought himself since coming to the Cape is a good casting rod. He said he's wanted a fishing pole ever since he was a kid."

And maybe if everything had gone well, the next thing he would have bought would have been a telescope.

"Bill," Cathy said, "I've done something I hope you won't mind. I'm letting Jed use your office."

"Jed Moriarty's using my office?" Bill was amused.

"Yes. I guess you haven't noticed, but it's been rainy the past couple of days and the forecast isn't great for the rest of the week. Jed needs to get his paperwork in order before I can determine what he should do."

Bill rolled his eyes. "Tell me about Moriarty's records."

"He hasn't had a chance to work on his books," Cathy said quickly. "He's been working straight out, trying to get a house under roof that he hopes to sell before winter."

"You don't have to defend him, Cathy." Bill's expression was quizzical. "I know he's been stretched for a long time. If his damned accountant hadn't been so greedy, Jed wouldn't have this problem now. Anyway, about my office..."

"Well, he was trying to work in his trailer, but his creditors kept calling and he couldn't get anything done. So it seemed logical to let him use your space for the time being."

"Good idea," Bill said approvingly.

"Everett doesn't think so."

"Oh?"

"Everett considers it highly unprofessional to allow a client to move onto the premises."

Bill made an impatient gesture. "Everett must have been raised on dill pickles."

Cathy laughed, and started telling Bill a couple of amusing stories about life in the office with Everett over the past few days. Bill had a few hospital tales of his own to tell.

They were still bantering when Beth Grant came back from dinner.

Beth was a tall, thin woman, with light brown hair and beautiful hazel eyes. She wasn't pretty, but she had a fantastic personality.

Cathy talked to Beth and Bill for a while, then said, "Next thing I know, your nurse will be throwing me out, Bill. I'd better leave or they won't let me in again."

The lights had been dimmed in the hospital lobby. Outside, the rain was coming down steadily. The world seemed to be awash as Cathy walked across the hospital parking lot, and her spirits felt as damp as the weather. Hospitals always depressed her. They reminded her of her mother's final illness. She had been twelve at the time, an impressionable age, and the hospital atmosphere had made a negative impact she still found hard to shake

She thought about seeking Gladys's company, maybe suggesting they go somewhere for a bite to eat. But as she pulled into her driveway, Cathy saw that the lights were out in Gladys's apartment. Probably Gladys was off playing in her cribbage tournament.

The house seemed lonely to Cathy. She poured herself a glass of wine, popped a TV dinner into the oven and was glad when the telephone pealed, breaking the silence. She hurried to answer it.

It was her father. "I'm in the mood for Cape Cod lobster. If you'll be free Saturday, suppose I come down? I can bring Eduardo along, if you like, and he can fix dinner for us. Or we can go out.''

"Dad, since I can have the lobsters cooked at the fish market, there really isn't any problem," Cathy pointed out. She frowned at the receiver. "Anyway, I *can* put a meal together, you know. I'm not the gourmet chef Eduardo is, but..."

The judge agreed to leave the matter of a lobster dinner in her hands. He also accepted her invitation to stay over at her house Saturday night, which she knew was exactly what he'd been angling for.

She had no sooner hung up on the judge than the phone rang again, and this time it was Frank Winslow.

"I'll be back in Boston next week," he said. "I thought if I could cut away for a while on Tuesday, I might rent a car and drive down to the Cape...provided you'll be free for lunch."

Cathy thought of her work schedule, and knew she wasn't going to be able to indulge in a leisurely lunch for a long time to come. On the other hand, she wanted to see Frank.

"I can eke out about an hour and a half, but not much more than that," she warned.

"Suppose I pick you up at your office on Tuesday at one o'clock and we won't go too far afield?"

By the time she finished talking to Frank, the TV dinner was overdone. Cathy washed her meal down with a second glass of wine, then showered and went to bed.

Rain greeted Cathy again when she woke up the next morning. And that, she told herself, meant that Jed

Moriarty would undoubtedly be working in Bill's office again today.

But he wasn't.

By noon, having checked Bill's office several times, Cathy buzzed the intercom. "Have you seen Moriarty?" she asked Gladys.

"No," Gladys said. "Should I have?"

"I would have thought he'd be here by now."

"Are you sure he's coming in today?"

She wasn't sure. And she reminded herself grimly that it was a mistake to take anything for granted where Jed Moriarty was concerned. He was very much his own person. Too damned much, she thought, irritated because there was no way he could be building in this kind of weather, which meant that he owed it to her, as well as to himself, to work on his accounts while he had this chance.

Cathy was disgruntled by the time she left the office. There had been no word from Moriarty. She'd checked his file, discovered she had his phone number, but she was damned if she was going to call him up. She gritted her teeth. The ball was in *his* court, dammit.

But by one o'clock the next afternoon, she was beginning to change her mind about that, and was thinking of reaching for the phone, when Jed Moriarty walked into her office.

Cathy had been so swamped with work that when Gladys went to lunch, she asked her to bring her back a sandwich. She was munching on ham and cheese on pumpernickel when Jed appeared, and when she saw him, she nearly choked.

He looked like hell. He also looked about as sexy as a man could look. He was wearing the yellow slicker, with the hood thrown back. His dark hair was damp, making it curlier than ever. He apparently had shaved hastily, and not close enough. There was a faint bluish stubble on his cheeks that came close to matching the dark shadows under his strained and bloodshot eyes.

"Where have you been?" Cathy demanded. Then, angry, she followed up with, "Did you go off on a bender?"

Jed glared at her. "Yeah," he drawled. "And it was a hell of a bender, all right."

He slumped into her client chair without waiting for an invitation, stretched out his long legs and eyed her with hostility that bristled.

"I can't stand it when people jump to lousy conclusions." His voice was tight. "And I resent the hell out of your attitude. I was sitting in my trailer on Cranberry Estates in Cedarville," he snapped.

"All this time?"

"Do you ever believe anybody? Yeah, all this time."

"You could have phoned," she accused.

He looked at Cathy as if she'd thrown him off base. "I didn't think it mattered," he admitted.

"Yes, it mattered." Cathy was working up her own head of steam. "I kept checking all day yesterday to see if you'd come in, and then again this morning...."

Jed was looking at her as if he were a child, and she was telling him a fairy tale. She softened, despite herself. "I was worried about you," she confessed.

She discovered that he sometimes did have the grace to look ashamed. He rubbed his eyes. "I'm sorry," he said. "I...I guess I'm not used to having anyone worry about me. It's never happened before."

Before she could fully react to that he added, "I couldn't have called you this morning, anyway."

"Your phone's out of order?"

"Yeah, I think you could say that. It's been ripped out of the wall. The phone company says there's no way they can get around to fixing it until Monday."

Cathy thought of her conversation with Bill, of Bill's gut feeling that Jed had an enemy.

"Jed . . ." She sat back and tried to suppress some of the fear that was fluttering inside her. "Will you please tell me what's happened?"

Jed slumped down farther. His legs looked incredibly long. He sighed and said reluctantly, "I stopped for something to eat on my way home Tuesday night. Up my way, there wasn't just a lot of rain, there was also a strong wind gusting. I was kind of restless, I had a hard time getting to sleep. I hadn't been asleep very long—it was about midnight, I guess—when I heard a loud crash.

"It was raining like hell. I got my slicker and a flashlight and went outside—"

"Why in the name of God didn't you call the police first?"

Jed's eyebrows lifted. "Why should I have called the police?"

"Jed, you've had trouble . . ."

"I put the crash down to the wind and the rain," Jed said. "And it looked like I was right, once I checked things out. There's a shed near my trailer where I keep tools and supplies. I would have sworn I'd locked the shed door, but evidently I hadn't because it was flapping back and forth."

"Is that what made the noise you heard?"

"No, that was a real crash. What caused it was a stack of windows I'd propped against the shed wall. They toppled over."

"Were they broken?"

"Most of them."

"Didn't it occur to you this might be vandalism? You've had other incidents—"

"Yes, there've been other incidents. I thought about vandalism . . . I'm not trying to shut my eyes to anything, Cathy. But there really was a gale wind blowing. It made sense that a sudden gust could have caused the whole thing.

"I admit I did feel sort of funny about it, regardless. So I decided to hang around yesterday. The only time I went out was in the early evening, when I went over to a place in the village to get something hot to eat. . . ."

He was driving her crazy. Cathy pressed impatiently, "Yes?"

"Someone broke into the trailer while I was out— which obviously meant there'd been someone around watching me, because I wasn't gone that long."

"What did they do?"

"They smashed some things up. I have a small TV. It was wrecked. My coffeemaker was smashed. A can of red paint had been upturned over the bed. It was all over the sheets and pillows. They looked like they were covered with blood."

Cathy went cold. "At that point, didn't you call the police?"

"I believe I mentioned that the telephone was ripped out of the wall."

Cathy pushed her phone across the desk to him. "Call the Cedarville cops now."

He shook his head. "No."

"Jed, this isn't the time to be stubborn."

"I'm not being stubborn, Cathy. The Cedarville cops have been watching *me* ever since my houses were set on fire last summer. Didn't I make it clear to you that *I'm* the one they suspect? The arson team that was called in, the insurance investigators, they've all been keeping an eye on me, waiting for me to slip, to make a mistake."

"Jed, that's paranoid."

"The hell it's paranoid. It's the truth. If you don't believe me, ask Bill Grant."

"I already have," Cathy said quietly.

"Then maybe you can see what the score is."

"The score doesn't add up as far as I'm concerned, Jed."

She saw him swallow. Then he said softly, "Thank you."

"I believe *you*," she said, "and I believe in you. So does Bill. Bill also thinks there's someone out there who has it in for you. At this point, you need to start considering that...before something really terrible happens."

Jed saw the concern in Cathy's beautiful topaz eyes, and told himself not to be a damned fool. Cathy was a generous and caring person; she'd be worried about any client who was in his predicament.

"I'm not saying there's no one in the world who may dislike me, Cathy. I am saying I don't think there's anyone who dislikes me enough to start this kind of a vendetta."

He was thinking of Angela's brothers—his three ex-brothers-in-law. And, they were "ex." Although Angela had died before she divorced him, any connection he'd ever had with her family had died with her. They had never liked him; even after Angela was dead, they had laid blame at his door for things and events over which he'd had no control and for which he was not responsible.

He'd never made real peace with Sam or Benny or Mario DiAngelo. But they had achieved a kind of truce, and all connections had been severed once he'd left Somerville and moved to the Cape.

Neither vandalism nor arson would be their style anyway. Not Sam's or Benny's certainly. Mario had always been a kind of loner, but even he . . .

"From now on," Jed told Cathy, "I intend to be a lot more careful and a lot more watchful. I also intend to set my own trap."

She wanted to shake him. "What do you think you are, Moriarty?" she demanded. "A one-man vigilante committee?"

"No. But I do have a lead. . . ."

Cathy sat up straight. "What are you talking about?"

"Now and then I've seen a pickup truck around my place that had no business being there."

"Did you tell the police this?"

"Yeah . . . back at the time of the fire. They took down the description. It's an old pickup, a dirty green. Once I got close enough to it so I could have read the license plate if it hadn't been crusted with dirt. The guy roared off. . . ."

"And the police haven't been able to find the truck?"

Jed shrugged. "I'm not sure they've bothered to look."

What was she going to do with him? Cathy's anxiety showed as she began, "Honestly, Moriarty—"

Before she knew what was happening, Jed was around her desk and clasping her shoulders.

"You're tight as a drum," he complained, gently massaging her tense muscles. "Look, I promise you, Cathy, I won't do anything stupid...."

He paused. There was so much more he wanted to say to her, but this wasn't the time.

He kept massaging her neck muscles, and gradually he felt her begin to relax. He held back the impulses that were straining at him, begging to be let free. Then he yielded as he kissed her soft amber hair. He let go of her, and said, "I'd better get to work, or I'll never have the stuff you need ready."

Cathy wanted to reach up and grab his hands and hold on. It took effort to watch him walk out of her office. He was tugging at her heartstrings, and the tug became even stronger when, later, she slipped into Bill's office between appointments to see how Jed was doing. He was slumped over Bill's desk, his dark head pillowed in his arms, and he was fast asleep.

Cathy stood for a while and watched him in silence, then forced herself to go back to work.

Usually the office was closed on Saturday, but there were so many leftover details to tie up on that October Saturday that Cathy went in.

Gladys was ahead of her, straightening files. After chastising her for not having taken the day off, Cathy asked impulsively, "How about coming over for lobster tonight?" Gladys, too, needed a break.

"Bribery," Gladys accused, her eyes twinkling. "What time do you want me?"

"Seven," Cathy said, and it didn't occur to her until much later that she'd forgotten to tell Gladys her father would be aboard. Due to a variety of circumstances, the two of them had never met.

Cathy called the fish market she patronized and asked them to cook four good-size lobsters, to be picked up late that afternoon. Then she sat back and pondered about why she was getting four lobsters for three people.

She was beginning to feel as if Jed Moriarty were with her even when he was miles away.

She peeked into Bill's office now and then to see if maybe Jed had come in to do some work. He hadn't.

As the day passed, she grew more and more worried about him. So okay, she told herself, he was a strong, extremely capable man. But he wasn't invincible. No one was.

She could imagine how he'd scoff if he knew that she was running scared. Very scared.

Well, she couldn't help herself. And Jed was still foremost in her thoughts as she stopped at the market for the lobsters, then trundled home.

Gladys came to dinner wearing jeans, a peach sweater, a purple raincoat, old sneakers and almost no makeup.

This was such a contrast to the elegant wardrobe Gladys usually dressed in, that Cathy was amused. But she'd said lobster, after all, and Gladys had dressed for a casual lobster dinner between friends.

She was unprepared for the horrified expression on Gladys's face when she walked into the kitchen and found the judge there.

The judge had just poured himself a drink. He was dressed in the ultimately proper Bostonian way—in a magnificently tailored dark gray suit with a pale gray shirt and a gray-and-black-striped tie.

Gladys's inherent poise came to the surface as the two of them were introduced, but as soon as she could manage it, she gave Cathy a long, reproachful look.

Cathy got the message. Gladys felt she'd had a dirty trick played on her, and Cathy couldn't really blame her. But it had never occurred to her that the judge was a *contemporary* of Gladys's, and Gladys might view him through different eyes than she did.

She was thankful when Gladys's irrepressible sense of humor won out. Gladys accepted the drink the judge mixed for her and settled in.

Cathy prevailed upon her father and Gladys to go into the living room while she got things together. Earlier, she had set the lobsters into the oven to keep warm. Now she put a small pan of butter onto the stove to melt, stuck some garlic bread into the microwave, then went into her tiny dining room and lit the candles on the table.

She'd bought a pot of chrysanthemums and was using it as a colorful centerpiece. The atmosphere created by candlelight and flowers was unintentionally romantic. Cathy thought about that as she glanced down and saw that she'd set the table with four places.

She was making Freudian slips all over the place.

She shook her head in self-reproof, and was about to remove the extra silverware when she heard a thump on the back door.

When she went to open the door, it seemed natural to find Jed Moriarty looking down at her.

"Cathy, I'm sorry," he began. "I tried to call you earlier...."

"I didn't get home till almost six."

Her eyes lingered on Jed. He was wearing his yellow slicker, and he looked ... fabulous.

As she watched him, she saw his eyes travel over her shoulder, and she turned. The judge was standing in the dining-room doorway.

"Come in," she invited Jed. "I want you to meet my father."

Jed's handsome features hid behind a closed expression. But when Cathy introduced the two men, he said politely, "Sir," and he and her father shook hands.

Five minutes later, the judge had made a drink for Jed, and Jed had been invited to share lobster.

Cathy held her breath until he accepted the invitation.

As they savored the lobster, the conversation first centered on Bill Grant, then merged into fishing.

"I've never done any fishing," Jed admitted, in answer to a question by the judge. "But—" he grinned "—I bought a great rod a while back."

"You're talking about surf casting?" the judge asked.

"Yes."

"I do some casting now and then, but basically I'm a lazy fisherman," the judge confessed. "I have a little hideaway up in Maine on a lake, and what I like is to get out in my boat and..."

The judge was off on one of his favorite subjects.

After a time, Gladys volunteered, "My husband and I used to go fishing whenever we had the chance. But it's been a long time since I baited a hook...."

Cathy felt slightly left out as she listened to the three of them. When she occasionally went up to the judge's camp with him, she usually curled up on his front porch with a mystery novel.

After a time, she got up and started to clear the table. She was putting lobster shells into a plastic bag when Jed appeared, carrying plates and utensils.

"You don't have to do that," she protested.

His smile made his eyes look like crown jewels. "Those two are talking about cribbage," he told her, nodding over his shoulder.

"How did they ever get on to *that?*"

"I don't know. The judge asked Gladys what she did for recreation, and Gladys mentioned she was playing in a cribbage tournament next week."

Cathy laughed. "Next to fishing or bridge, my father would rather play cribbage than do anything else."

"He's a great guy, Cathy."

She was twisting a fastener around the plastic bag. "Thank you. Most of the time I have to agree with you."

"Be glad you have a father like that."

"I am."

She dumped the cutlery Jed handed her into soapy water, and dared to say, "You said you were fourteen when you lost your father, didn't you, Jed?"

"Yes."

"What happened?"

"He was shot in a liquor-store holdup."

"He was a police officer?"

"No," Jed said, "he was a thief."

He saw her shock.

"My mother used to worry that I might turn out to be a chip off the old block," he said quietly. "My older brother got in trouble with the cops early on. They gave him a chance to go into the service to get off the hook, and he took it. He was killed in Vietnam."

Cathy didn't know what to say to him.

Before she could say anything, he'd gone back into the dining room to get more dishes.

Cathy made coffee, and dug out a box of fancy cookies. Jed lingered awhile, then said regretfully, "I guess I'd better take off."

Cathy thought about him going back to the trailer in Cedarville, and shivered.

"I should get home, too," Gladys announced.

Cathy had been watching her father and Gladys. Now she wished perhaps her father would tell Gladys he hoped he'd see her again.

He didn't. He merely said good-night.

Gladys slipped out the back door. Jed lingered on the threshold.

Rain still slanted down. He cast a glance at the big drops plopping on the driveway beyond the back light Cathy had switched on, and said, "Doesn't seem like this is ever going to let up."

He smacked his forehead. "That reminds me. I nearly forgot why I came over here. I left my stuff in Bill's office, and I wonder if it would be possible for me to stop by and pick it up so I can work on it tomorrow. Is there a night watchman in the building who would let me in if you phoned him?"

"That won't be necessary," Cathy said. "I'll give you a key to the staff entrance. But why take everything back to your place, Jed? Why not work at the office tomorrow? You'll have the place to yourself—

no interruptions. You should be able to make a lot of headway."

Before he could comment on that, Cathy went into the living room and got her extra set of office keys out of a desk drawer. As she handed them to Jed, he said, "I appreciate this kind of trust, Cathy."

She was tempted to tell him she'd trust him with anything. Instead, she began tentatively, "Jed...?"

He waited.

"Did anything happen at your place last night?"

"No. I do have floodlights around. I kept them on all night. That may raise hell with my electric bill, but I felt it was a precaution I needed to take."

She tugged at the sleeve of the yellow slicker. "Be careful, will you?"

"Cathy, don't worry."

Her smile was strained. "I'll worry."

Jed's eyes darkened as he stared down at her, and for a moment he looked stunned. Then he leaned over and brushed her forehead with his lips.

"I'll be okay," he said softly. "I'll call you tomorrow."

"Promise?"

Jed nodded, and slipped off into the night, turning up his face so that the pelting rain chilled his skin.

This was nature's version of a cold shower—and he needed it.

Chapter Six

The judge was too sharp.

"Did I hear you tell that young man you were going to give him the key to your *office?*" he asked Cathy.

"You were eavesdropping," she accused.

"No, I just have good hearing. Catherine, is Jed Moriarty the client who is considering filing Chapter 11?"

"Now why would you think that?"

"You mentioned at the dinner table that he's actually Bill Grant's client. Then Jed said he'd bought a fishing rod as soon as he moved to the Cape, but he's never had a chance to use it. That indicated to me that he's had his hands full."

"Couldn't that simply mean that he's been extremely busy?"

"Judges tend to develop a certain intuition, my dear."

Irritated, Cathy snapped, "That's a categorical statement if I ever heard one."

"Cathy, *is* Jed Moriarty about to file Chapter 11?"

Cathy cast a baleful eye at her father. "Does that really concern you?"

"Perhaps I could be helpful," the judge suggested mildly.

"Dad, you've never handled bankruptcy cases."

"True. But I like Jed Moriarty, and I'd say he's a man with determination, purpose and courage."

Cathy wondered if she were hearing her father correctly. He didn't make statements like that, especially about someone he'd just met.

"How did he get into his present predicament?" the judge asked.

"A combination of factors, I'd say. The same kinds of things have been happening to him that have happened to people all over the country."

"Does he have an option other than to file Chapter 11?"

"That's what I'm trying to figure out."

Cathy sighed. Fatigue and frustration were catching up with her, and the last thing she needed was to get into a legal discussion with her father.

"Your Honor," she announced, "I am going to bed. What about you?"

"I think I'll watch the late news. Do you still have some of that excellent French brandy?"

Cathy gave the judge the brandy bottle and a snifter, then headed upstairs.

* * *

Judge Merrill left for Boston late Sunday morning. Cathy scanned the *Globe* while listening for the phone, which refused to ring.

By the middle of the afternoon, she was wondering whether Jed had ever made it to Hyannis, or whether something else had happened in Cranberry Estates.

She wrestled with her better judgment, then said aloud, "Oh, the hell with it," put on some rain gear and drove to her office. Jed's red pickup was parked close to the staff door.

Cathy made straight for Bill Grant's sanctum, but when she walked in, it seemed to her that Jed wasn't doing much beyond staring into space. Then she saw the angry bruise on his chin, and she felt the cutting edge of sharp fear.

"What went on this time?" she demanded.

"I tripped over a barrier," he growled.

"How did that happen?"

"There was someone hanging around the trailer again last night," he admitted reluctantly. "Despite the pouring rain, I heard sounds that could only have been made by a human. Whoever it was, banged into something. I heard him howl and then curse."

"What did you do?"

"I took off after him."

Jed grimaced. "I guess I should say I *tried* to take off after him. It was pretty murky. I had a flashlight, but I didn't want to use it. I was following sound, and the guy was pretty noisy.

"After a few minutes, I heard a car door bang and a motor start up. Heavy throb—I was pretty sure it must be that same pickup. I got the bright idea of detouring down a path that comes out farther along the main development road. I was going to intercept him if I could and take it from there. I thought that even if I couldn't connect with him, I should at least be able to get close enough so I could use the flashlight and make out his license plate number. That didn't happen.''

He was driving her crazy. ''Damn it, Jed,'' she exploded, ''what *did* happen?''

''There was a wooden barrier in the middle of the path. I didn't even see it until I was on top of it. I went flying over it, and banged the hell out of my chin. The worst of it is that the guy must have set up the barrier before he came close to the trailer. That shows how well he knows his way around my place.''

''You're sure the barrier wasn't already there?''

''Of course I'm sure. I use that path all the time.''

''I can't believe you'd be idiotic enough to go after a man *and* a truck by yourself, under those circumstances.''

She studied the bruise on his chin. ''You ought to have someone take a look at that,'' she advised. ''Why don't we go over to the hospital emergency room?''

He gave her a scathing glance. ''The chin is fine. I spent the rest of the night putting ice on it.''

Cathy sat down and stared at him helplessly. ''Must you always be so stubborn?'' she demanded. ''You seem to think it's a crime to let anyone try to help you.''

He looked a little bit sheepish, but he only said, ''I don't need to do anything about the chin, Cathy.''

''If you say so. But it makes sense to me that you have to start taking some precautions, Jed. Even get yourself a gun, maybe.''

His face was stony. "I will never get a gun. I *hate* guns."

When she remembered what he had told her about both his father and his brother, Cathy could see why.

She couldn't let up on him, though. "You've said you don't think there's anyone out there who would be enough against you to do these things," she said. "Hasn't it begun to occur to you that maybe you're wrong? It's about time for you to do some in-depth thinking, search your memory...."

Jed stirred restlessly. "Do you suppose we could get out of here and go somewhere?" he hedged. "Could I buy you a drink?"

Cathy decided that her best option was to hole up with him someplace and try to talk some sense into him. So she said, "I guess so."

"Your car or my pickup?" he asked her, as they left the building and paused under the roof overhang before dashing out through the rain.

"Why don't we take my car?"

"Okay."

"You drive," she said. "If you don't mind, that is."

"Something wrong?" he asked quickly.

"No." She pushed her hair back from her temples. She felt unhinged, she was getting a headache, she was worried to death about this obstinate man standing next to her; aside from all of that, everything was just fine.

She took another look at the bruise on Jed's face. It seemed to her it was getting even larger and uglier; it made her wince to look at it.

Cathy shuddered.

She *felt* Jed's eyes on her, and turned to see him studying her intently.

"What's bugging you, Cathy?" he asked her. "Maybe you've had enough of me for a while. Would you rather not go anywhere right now? It might be better for you go home and get some rest. I'd understand that."

"Well, don't be so understanding," she said crossly, sure he wanted to get off the hook so he wouldn't have to level with her. She tried to press her point. "Jed, doesn't it even occur to you that you could have been hurt seriously last night? I mean *really* hurt."

"Yes," he said quietly, "that occurred to me. I know now that I was careless. I acted before I thought things through. That won't happen again."

"Jed, the aggressor always has the advantage over the victim. The element of surprise, if nothing else. Didn't anyone ever tell you that?"

Why was he looking at her so *tenderly?* Cathy saw his slight but indulgent smile and bristled. He was acting as if danger were a figment of her imagination.

She said abruptly, "How about buying me that drink you promised?"

By way of answer, he grabbed her hand, and the two of them raced through the steady drizzle to her car.

The small café Jed took her to was almost deserted at that hour on a Sunday afternoon. They settled into a booth, and to Jed's surprise, Cathy ordered a beer, just as he did. Then she nervously munched on the pretzels the waitress brought them.

Jed watched her, saw her nervousness and finally said, "I'll ask again. What's bugging you, Cathy?"

She snapped a pretzel in several pieces, then sputtered, "You."

His eyes clouded. He said, "I'm sorry. I'm not trying to give you a bad time. That's the last thing I want to do."

"It's not a question of giving me a bad time."

Cathy, Jed saw, wasn't even trying to hide her anxiety, and that surprised him. What had happened to his cool, levelheaded attorney?

She put the pretzel fragments in an ashtray, and Jed suspected maybe she'd asked herself the same question. She was more composed as she said, "Someone needs to point out to you that this is risky business you're dealing with, and I appear to be elected."

She leaned forward. She was wearing a loose, bulky sweater that had a vee neck. Jed got a tantalizing glimpse of creamy flesh, he saw the provocative swell of her breasts and he smelled the light but sexy scent she was wearing as it wafted toward him.

He felt as if he could get drunk just by looking and sniffing. How could she expect him to concentrate on anything when she was coming on to him like this...even unintentionally?

She broke another pretzel, then said, "Let's get back to the subject of enemies. Who hates you, Moriarty?"

Jed nearly laughed out loud. Cathy had a habit of using his last name when she was trying to be impersonal, but it was no longer working very well.

She repeated her question. "Who?" she persisted.

He said honestly, "I already told you I don't think anyone *hates* me, Cathy. My three ex-brothers-in-law are not crazy about me. But that's a long way from hate."

"Okay, let's say they don't hate you. That doesn't mean they may not dislike you . . . intensely. Tell me why."

"It's a long story," Jed answered evasively.

"We can take the rest of the day. This place isn't doing a landslide business. I don't think they'll throw us out."

Jed had never wanted to get into any of this with her. He had never wanted to dredge up the past. His present was bad enough, he thought now. What he'd been hoping was that he could hurdle the present and maybe latch on to a green light for the future. Then . . .

He hadn't let himself go beyond the "then" where Cathy was concerned, because there were too many things to consider and too many of *them* were negative. He would be an idiot, Jed reminded himself, to become so blinded by Cathy that he forgot about the differences between them. Those differences were not going to melt away.

"Jed," Cathy persisted, "stop holding out on me, will you? I need to know about your brothers-in-law."

Jed cursed silently. Why had this had to happen? Anything he told her about his past was only going to deepen those differences he'd been thinking about.

He said slowly, "They hold me responsible—at least they did—for some things that were not my fault."

"Such as?"

"Hell, it's complicated, Cathy. Anyway, this was all back in Somerville. It doesn't have anything to do with anything here."

God, he wished she'd buy that. Believe it.

"Somerville is less than a two-hour drive from here, Jed," Cathy informed him. "So how can you be so sure?"

"Because everything that happened then might as well have been in another life." He had to convince her of that. "*They* know that as well as I do. What went down in Somerville has nothing to do with what's been going down here."

"Suppose you give me a few facts and let me decide that."

Jed knotted his fingers together, twisted them. "What do you want to know?"

Cathy felt as if she were being pulled in two directions. She needed to know everything, but she was afraid to hear anything. Whatever Jed told her was bound to introduce a new dimension between them. He was going to have to talk about his dead wife....

She felt a stab of jealousy she couldn't push away.

She sounded grim as she said, "You told me about your father's death, and you said your brother had been killed in Vietnam. I can't remember whether you mentioned this, or whether it was in something Bill had written down. But, at some point, you and your mother moved out of the place where you were living, right?"

Where you used to sneak out at night and watch the stars.

He nodded. "Ever since I could remember, my mother worked, even though she had terrible arthritis. She kept on working until it got so bad it was all she could do to walk.

"She was determined that I stay in school and get as much education as I could. I worked after school and on Saturdays and Sundays, as well. But there was no way I could bring in enough with part-time jobs to support the two of us.

"Finally, she had to turn to her brother, Mike, who was all she had. He was a contractor there in Somerville, married, and he had a couple of daughters but no sons. He took us in, and I went to work for him and finished high school at night—thanks to my mother's prodding. My uncle would just as soon I dropped out.

"I paid my uncle room and board for my mother and myself. I tried to save enough so we could move out and get a place of our own. But the money wouldn't stretch that far."

Jed beckoned the waitress to bring him another beer. Cathy still had more than half of hers. He knew the worst part of his recital was yet to come. He gritted his teeth, then plunged into it.

"My mother died when I was twenty. A while after that, my uncle had a chance to merge his business with Tony DiAngelo's. Tony had a successful contracting business, and his hands were in a few other pies, as well. After the merger, I worked primarily for Tony.

"Tony DiAngelo had three sons. Sam and Benny were in college by then. Mario was still in high school. And there was his daughter, Angela."

Jed paused. His voice had been getting lower and lower; he sounded husky by the time he spoke Angela's name.

Cathy reached for another pretzel and snapped it into pieces. She didn't want to look at Jed. She heard the misery in his voice; she didn't want to see it reflected in his face.

"Angela was nineteen when I met her," he said. "I was twenty-two. We...fell in love." Jed slid over that as quickly as he could.

"Tony didn't approve," he went on. "He wanted Angela to do better. He wanted her to marry the son of one of his business associates who was a few years older, had money and good prospects...."

Jed set his beer mug down on the table with a thud. "When Tony began to put the pressure on," he said, "Angela and I eloped. That was twelve years ago.

"Our marriage was the first thing Angela's father and her brothers held against me. After that... Hell, Cathy, it's all ancient history now."

Cathy still couldn't look at him. She was having a hard time trying to suppress the picture of Angela DiAngelo that was forming in her mind.

She was sure Angela must have been beautiful. A gorgeous Italian girl with raven hair that spilled over her shoulders, eloquent dark eyes and a sexy, voluptuous figure that would drive a man crazy.

She could imagine how madly in love Jed must have been with Angela. It hurt like hell to think of the intense passion that must have flared between the two of them. Deep down in Cathy's chest, the pain throbbed....

She had to force herself to say, "You need to spell out the ancient history for me, Jed."

Jed said tightly, "Okay, we didn't give Tony the grandchildren he wanted, and I am *not* about to go into the reasons why. Regardless, Tony blamed me because the years went by and he didn't become a grandfather. Tony was blind to a lot of things, which doesn't matter anymore. What it came down to was that the marriage didn't work. We went on for nine whole hellish years, then Angela left me. She ran off with another man and the two of them were killed. Tony and the brothers blamed me for *that*, too. They said it would never have happened if I'd been a decent husband to her. Is that enough?''

Cathy felt as if she were going to choke. "No," she said.

"All right, I inherited money from Angela. Tony and the brothers were infuriated by my benefiting from Angela's death, but they had no legal grounds to stand on. By then, Tony had fired me and I was working for someone else. Tony was like a crazy man at that point. He had idolized Angela. Before long, he had a stroke that killed him...and the brothers laid the blame for that on me, too. But everything they felt against me then stemmed from grief, Cathy. They got over it.

"When Tony's kids were born, he took out a big insurance policy on each of them. That's the money that came to me from Angela. God knows I didn't want to take it, but then I saw it was my big chance to get out of Somerville and begin a life of my own.

"I vowed I'd pay every cent of it back one day—either to the DiAngelos, or to some charity. Maybe that will still come to pass, maybe it won't. Regardless, coming to the Cape was the best thing that ever happened to me. Now...can we get the hell out of here, counselor?''

Jed slapped a bill down on the table and anchored it with an ashtray.

As they got up to walk out, Cathy felt as if the tension between the two of them was so thick, it would need an ax to chop through it. Jed halted her inside the small vestibule of the café, and put a hand on her shoulder. Then, when she turned toward him, he gently tugged her raincoat hood over her hair.

"Cathy—" his voice was so low she had to strain to hear it "—it wasn't that I wanted to hold out on you. It's just that I hate like hell to talk about the things that happened in my life before I came to the Cape. That was another existence. It's all behind me, and that's where I want to keep it."

"If the DiAngelo brothers still have it in for you, you're not going to be able to bury everything that happened, Jed."

A poor choice of words, she thought, as soon as she'd spoken. A very poor choice of words.

She said quickly, "I think we should have them checked out."

"Even if you're right—and though this may annoy you, I don't think you are—that would require hiring a private detective, Cathy. I don't have that kind of money."

"If you ever hope to collect on your fire insurance, you're going to have to get yourself off the hook," Cathy reminded him.

"I know that," Jed agreed, "but I'll have to do it another way. As I see it, the way I can get myself off the hook is by trapping the guy who's been sneaking around my place and raising hell."

"That is just too dangerous," she protested sharply. "Do you *want* to get yourself killed?"

"No," he said, and the force of the negative compelled her to look at him.

His eyes were dark right now, intent. "My life has never seemed so valuable to me before," he told her. "I want to get out of this mess I'm in, then I want to do my damnedest to make up for lost time so I can...live."

He didn't dare say anything more than that to her.

Jed opened the door, and she went through it. Outside, the rain slanted down, a wet gray curtain between them and the rest of the world. Jed took her arm, intending to guide her. But he felt her stiffen, and he very nearly let go of her.

Had she been so turned off by what he'd said that she didn't even want him to touch her?

He was unprepared when Cathy swung around and threw her arms around his neck. She stood on tiptoe, tilting her head so that she could reach for his lips.

He helped her, bent over. Their mouths fused, and Jed was rocked by the intensity of her kiss. He sensed that she was putting her fears for him into a tangible expression that aimed straight for his heart, and he was staggered.

He'd had a lot of lessons in self-control. What he hadn't realized was how fast those lessons could be forgotten. The heat that surged through him became a flame that ignited the core of his need, then spread through his veins and on, until every atom in his body was on fire. His logic crumbled. The way he wanted Cathy went beyond reason.

He pulled her closer, molding her body against his, letting her feel the force of his arousal. His lips nibbled, sucked, licked; he felt the thrust of her tongue, and his deep shudder was convulsive.

God, how he wanted her! He wanted to show her through his actions what he couldn't tell her in words. He wanted to let caring mixed with passion speak for him; he wanted to make love to her all through this rainy night and beyond, past the dawn. He wanted to put everything he'd ever felt and ever could feel into that lovemaking. Taking, yes, but giving even more....

When a car turned into the parking lot and headlights cut through the rain, the pain of denial was torture. But he had to let her go.

Their mood was shattered by the time they pulled up in back of Cathy's office.

Jed, one hand on the car door, said, "If you don't object, I think I'll go back in and try to finish up."

He felt as though he had a sore throat, and his voice rasped.

"Why not wait till tomorrow so you can get a fresh start?" Cathy sounded almost as hoarse.

"I heard a weather report earlier. It's supposed to clear."

Jed's eyes lingered on Cathy's face, and he clenched the office key until it dug into his palm. "You still look tired," he told her, "and you probably have a blockbuster week ahead of you. Try to get some rest, okay?"

Jed didn't wait for her answer. He gave her hand a quick squeeze, mumbled good-night and left while he still had just enough strength to move away from her.

The sun was shining the next morning. Cathy looked up at the morning sky and she swore.

With good weather, Jed definitely would go back to work. And she wished, instead, that he would be around today so that she could talk to him again about getting in touch with the police.

She was tempted to call the Cedarville police chief herself, introduce herself as Jed's attorney, then take it from there. But she could immediately think of two reasons why she shouldn't do that. For one thing, Jed would be furious at what he was certain to consider an invasion of his privacy, whether or not she was his legal representative. For another, it would make more sense to discuss this with Bill Grant first. He had spoken to a private investigator who was working for Jed's insurance company. The investigator might be the person to contact first, and Bill would know about that.

Cathy got to her office before either Gladys or Everett, and the first thing she saw was a neat folder in the middle of her blotter with her name scrawled across the face of it.

She opened it, and began to scan the information Jed had left for her. As she read, she had to admit that she hoped she could find some fault with what he'd done; some omissions, maybe, or errors, or discrepancies.

She couldn't. Left alone, with peace and quiet in which to work, Jed had done an excellent job. By the time she finished what he had noted for her, there was no room left for doubt. She knew that with the information contained in these pages, she had everything she needed to decide on the course of action he should take.

Now she had no reason to get in touch with him until she'd done some homework herself. And obviously it was wrong to feel disappointed because he'd given her so exactly what she wanted . . . where information was concerned.

It was a relief when nine o'clock came, and Gladys ushered in the first client.

The day passed, and it was so filled with a variety of complex legal work that it was late in the afternoon before Cathy had the chance to ask Gladys the question that had been plaguing her.

With the last client gone, she went out to the reception room and paused by Gladys's desk. She tried to sound casual as she queried, "Has Jed set up another appointment with you?"

"No," Gladys said. "Should he have?"

"Yes, I would think so."

Gladys heard the testiness in Cathy's voice and looked up at her boss, surprised.

"Something wrong?" she asked.

The words burst out of Cathy. "Jed is being... just plain damned stubborn."

"What has he done?"

"It isn't so much what he's done, it's what he hasn't done."

As she spoke, it occurred to Cathy that Gladys didn't know anything about the vandalism at Cranberry Estates. She hadn't seen the ugly bruise on Jed's face. She wasn't aware that he flatly refused to seek assistance from people who could help him...especially the police.

The man was more stubborn than a mule.

Cathy made a sudden decision. "Look, Gladys," she said, "if Jed does call here for an appointment, don't do him any special favors. Just let him wait his turn with the others."

Gladys cast a skeptical eye at her employer. "All right, if you say so."

"I say so." Cathy headed for her office before she could change her mind.

Chapter Seven

"You look wonderful," Frank Winslow said.

He had booked a window table at a lovely old inn overlooking Nantucket Sound. He'd wanted to order champagne in celebration of their reunion, but Cathy deterred him.

"I have a heavy workload this afternoon," she reminded him. "I can't risk going back to the office feeling fuzzy."

Now Frank was sipping Scotch, and Cathy was drinking ginger ale. But she obligingly clicked her glass with his and echoed, "To being together again." Then she wondered just what he meant by "together."

Frank's light blue eyes surveyed her appreciatively. "I can't believe it's been twelve years," he said.

Twelve years. Cathy remembered Jed telling her that he'd married Angela DiAngelo twelve years ago. At just about that time, give or take a couple of months, she'd been graduating from law school and, simultaneously, she and Frank had broken off their relationship.

Frank had finally told her about his plans to wed his former high school sweetheart come September.

Cathy had realized, long ago, that her pride had been more hurt than her heart by his revelation. Even so, she didn't look back on her law school graduation day with fond memories. She had been bitterly conscious of Frank sitting on the same stage a row or so away from her.

She hadn't seen him since that graduation day. Now she took a close look at him while he was absorbed in studying the menu. He was as handsome as ever. Tall, blond, with an even, golden tan and a casual confidence that came from having a background of family money, private schooling and social graces.

Over the years, news about him had drifted to her from mutual friends. She knew he was doing well in his profession. And she suspected that he might be in the marriage market again. She was prepared to have him try to convince her that the past was the past, to tell her he'd made a grave mistake and it was time now for them to get together again. They were so right for each other.

She knew him well. Frank didn't waste time on people, activities, anything that wasn't generated for a purpose.

Yes, she decided, Frank hadn't detoured to Cape Cod during his business trip to Boston just to say hello to her. That wouldn't be his style.

Cathy ordered a salad. Frank ordered a lobster dish that was a specialty of the house. Then he sat back and said, "Tell me about yourself."

Cathy had to smile. She thought about her current office scene—tangling with Everett, visiting Bill in the hospital, chatting with Gladys, keeping up with the judge . . . and Jed Moriarty.

She said honestly, "Just now, that would be much too complicated a story."

Frank looked interested, so she added quickly, "Anyway, I would much rather hear about you."

He jiggled the ice in the glass he was holding, and smiled ruefully. "I lead a dull life."

"Come on, Frank," Cathy protested.

"I do lead a dull life. I've been a bachelor for the past three years, Cathy. You knew Maura and I had divorced?"

"I'd heard, yes," she admitted.

"No point in going into that. She remarried over a year ago. She has custody of the kids. . . ."

"You have two children?" She'd heard that, too.

He nodded. "Evan is ten, Judy is seven. I get them on holidays and for a while during the summer. Maura lives in Idaho now, so there are no weekend visits with the kids.

"I have a condo in Rosslyn—the Virginia side of the Potomac," he went on. "A fairly easy commute to work. Actually, I travel quite a bit."

Cathy led him into telling her about just what he did in the Justice Department, and the time she'd allotted for their lunch sped by.

It was a couple of minutes after two-thirty when they pulled into the parking lot back of Cathy's office, and Frank walked her to the staff door.

He looked down at her and smiled tenderly. "This has really been great," he said. "I expect to get back to Boston a couple of times between now and Christmas. But how about you coming down to Washington some weekend and letting me give you the nation's capital on a silver platter?''

"I can't make any plans till the office gets back on an even keel," Cathy told him quickly.

"I understand that."

There was a soft light in Frank's pale blue eyes. "I can wait," he said. Then he swiftly drew Cathy into his arms and kissed her.

Jed Moriarty had just brought his pickup truck to a stop at the back of the parking lot.

He had remembered a while ago that he still had a key to Cathy's office, and he thought he should return it. He also needed to make another appointment with her, and had decided he could set that up with Gladys at the same time.

Now he saw Cathy in another man's arms, and he felt as if he'd been hit a hard blow right in the middle of his stomach. The air went out of him. For a second he actually doubled up. By the time he straightened, Cathy had gone into the building, and her date was opening the door of a dark-colored sedan.

Jed didn't move until Cathy's date had driven off. Then he roared out of the parking lot, furious with Cathy, with himself, and jealous as hell.

Though he tried for the rest of the afternoon to tell himself that he was being incredibly stupid, it didn't work.

For Cathy, the afternoon was turning out to be miserable. Each of her clients seemed to be more difficult than the previous one and, between clients, Everett was giving her even more grief than usual.

To add to that, there was no word from Jed, and she kept thinking about him working by himself over in his development.

He was alone, and anything could happen to him under the present circumstances. If he were hurt it could be hours, days, before anyone found him....

Right in the middle of a conference with one of her clients, Cathy buzzed Gladys and said, "Give Moriarty a call, will you? I just want to be sure he's okay. If you get his answering machine, leave a message and ask him to call."

"Will do," Gladys said, not quite able to camouflage her surprise.

When the client had left, Gladys came into the office to say, "Jed doesn't answer."

Cathy reached for her gold pen and rolled it between her fingers. "Did you leave a message on his machine?"

"His machine isn't turned on."

Cathy frowned. "That's strange. His phone *is* back in service, isn't it?"

"Yes."

"Then ..."

"Cathy—" Gladys's voice was gentle "—why are you so worried about him?"

"Because he's an idiot," Cathy snapped, and was astonished to feel hot tears stinging her eyes.

Gladys advanced into the room. "My dear," she began, "I think Jed has more sense than you give him credit for. I don't know what's happened to cause you so much concern, but—"

Cathy held up her hand. "Please! No lectures, Gladys. Now, show in the next client, will you?"

Long habit helped her concentrate on the practice of law for the balance of the afternoon. But when, late in the day, Everett appeared to register a complaint about what he called Gladys's "cavalier attitude," the lioness in Cathy came out of hiding, and she roared at him.

Everett retreated to lick his wounds in private.

Cathy stalked out of the building shortly after six, having pocketed her pride sufficiently to try Jed Moriarty's phone number twice, herself. There still was no answer.

She sat in her car feeling worried, resentful and totally out of sorts with everyone and everything. She didn't want to go home, she didn't want to go out to dinner, she didn't want to go to the movies....

She settled for driving over to the hospital and paying Bill Grant a visit.

Her delight at seeing Bill sitting up in a wheelchair, unhooked from most of the machines that had been holding him down, temporarily improved her mood, but only temporarily.

Beth Grant had been about to leave. She smiled at Cathy and said, "I'll put him in your hands."

"I doubt he'd want to be in them," Cathy muttered.

Beth, preoccupied with kissing her husband goodnight, didn't hear her. But Bill did, and once his wife had left he asked, "What was that all about?"

"Your client is driving me crazy," Cathy said explosively.

Bill grinned. "What has Moriarty done now, Cathy?"

"He is absolutely impossible, totally unreasonable," Cathy began...and at that moment the impossible, unreasonable man walked into the room.

Cathy knew he'd heard her. Their eyes met, and some sparks flew. Raw fury was stamped on Jed's face.

What had she done to him to provoke that kind of anger?

He actually swerved, and she was sure he was going to walk right out of the room. But Bill forestalled that.

"Hey," Bill said, "this is a rare opportunity." He grinned. "Why don't the two of you pull up chairs, and we can have a conference?"

"Thank you, but no thank you," Cathy said, before Jed could say anything. "I've had my fill of the law for one day."

She managed to smile at Bill. "It's great to see you on wheels. Next thing we know you'll be on your feet. After that, you can come back to the office and *I'll* take a vacation."

She bent over and kissed Bill on the forehead.

"Hey," Bill protested, "what's your hurry? You just got here."

"I only wanted to say hi." She'd never been any good at fibbing, but even if she were, Bill knew her too well to be fooled.

Bill raised a skeptical eyebrow. But he only said, "Okay, Jed, looks like we're stuck with each other."

Jed cleared his throat. "I just wanted to stop by to check up on you," he told Bill. He looked extremely uncomfortable. "I'll come back tomorrow, okay?"

Bill laughed. "Okay, kids. Go with my blessing."

Cathy was surprised to see Jed actually flush. Her cheeks didn't feel any too cool, for that matter.

She tried to get out of Bill's room before Jed did, and when she heard him right behind her, she gave thought to cutting down the stairs instead of waiting for the elevator. But that, she told herself, would look ridiculous.

Her bad mood lingered, though, and in a way seeing Jed hale and hearty had made it worse instead of better. Even the bruise on his chin had faded, as if to demonstrate to her that he didn't need her ministrations.

The elevator door opened. Cathy got in, Jed followed her and they stood next to each other in stony silence as the elevator descended to the lobby. Then Cathy said politely, "Good night," and started for the front entrance.

Jed caught up with her in a single stride and grabbed her arm.

His grip was strong; she felt as if she had an iron fist clutching her. She said irritably, "Let up a little, will you? I bruise easily."

He loosened his hold, but he didn't let go of her.

"I want to talk to you," he said.

She faced him, her eyes ablaze with suppressed anger. "This isn't a very good place to make conversation," she pointed out.

"I agree. Where shall we go?"

"I don't want to go anywhere right now except home," she said. "I'm tired. I've had enough of just about everything for one day."

"I can imagine," Jed said dryly.

"What's that supposed to mean?" she asked suspiciously.

"Was that Frank Winslow with you today? Or another one of your friends?"

She stared at him. "Have you been following me?"

"No," he snarled. "Of course not. I happened to pull into the lot back of your office when he was kissing you, that's all. I wanted to return your key."

Jed fished in his pants pocket, then held the key out to her. "Here."

She made no move to take it. "What stopped you earlier?" she asked.

"You mean, why didn't I walk into your place and give you back the key then? Let's just say my mood changed."

His mouth was tight, but as she looked at him, Cathy couldn't say that he looked impassive, though she didn't doubt that was what he was trying to do.

She felt a mischievous twinge of pure delight. Till very recently, Jed had seemed to find it so easy to pull down a curtain over his face. Now he was having a hard time hiding his feelings from her.

He hadn't liked watching Frank kiss her goodbye. He looked...jealous. There was no logical reason why that should please her so much, but it did.

Visitors were coming into the hospital. Jed and Cathy moved to one side to let them by. And it was then that Cathy saw the little girl staring rapturously at the dolls in a glass cabinet that stood at the edge of the hospital lobby.

Jed was still holding the office key, and was about to offer it to her again when he saw her face. She was staring at a small blond child as if she were seeing a vision.

He asked uncertainly, "Cathy?"

Cathy didn't answer him.

A woman who looked so much like the little girl— she had to be the mother—joined the child, and started to explain to her why they couldn't buy one of the dolls just then.

Cathy said softly. "She's adorable, isn't she?"

Puzzled by Cathy's change in attitude, Jed nodded. "Yes, she is."

As the woman and the child moved away, Cathy asked, "Did you ever wish you'd had children, Jed?"

Had he ever wished he had kids? A long-suppressed bitterness resurfaced, and he said abruptly, "At one time, yes."

"You're still not too old. I mean, one day you'll probably marry again, and—"

He ground out, "I'm in no position to marry anyone, Cathy, and the way things are going, there's no telling if I ever will be."

"At least," she said, "time is on your side."

Just what the hell was she getting at?

He was missing something here, Jed told himself, because it seemed to him right now that time definitely was not on his side.

Matter of fact, he'd been pushing the thoughts of *any* future away, ever since he'd left Cathy out in the office parking lot Sunday. He had all he could do to deal with what was happening right now.

"Was the stuff I left on your desk what you needed?" he asked her, suddenly changing the subject.

She looked at him as if he'd shaken her awake, and it took a minute for her to snap into the present.

Then she said, "Yes. I think you've covered everything."

"I didn't know when you'd have time to go through it, so I planned to ask Gladys today when you might want to see me again."

She smiled faintly. "When you dropped off the key?"

His grin was skewed. "Yeah."

"Frank is an old...friend," Cathy said. And added, "He'll never be more than a friend to me."

Now why had she needed to tell Jed that?

"I imagine you have a lot of...friends around," Jed suggested.

"Not really. But I imagine the same thing about you."

He shook his head. "There isn't anyone, Cathy."

Now why in *hell* had he felt the need to spell that out to Cathy? Jed asked himself.

"Look," he said, "I haven't had dinner yet. Have you?"

"No."

"Do you like Chinese food? There's a place just a few blocks from here...."

She shook her head. "I do like Chinese food, but I'm just too tired to go anywhere tonight, Jed. I intend to settle for a can of soup when I get home."

Jed scanned her lovely face. She did look tired, too tired, and also too vulnerable. He remembered the first time he'd met up with her in her office. She had seemed so unflappable to him—cool, competent, beautiful, fashionable. The prototype of an extremely successful career woman.

She was still all of that, of course. But right now her lipstick was smudged, probably from kissing Bill good-night, fatigue shadowed her eyes and her beautiful bronze hair hung in loose waves around her shoulders, making her look younger and so incredibly desirable that it was all Jed could do not to groan aloud.

It had taken all of his strength and self-control to leave her on Sunday. Now he wasn't sure he had enough left to do that again. Never in his life had he wanted anyone the way he wanted Cathy. His need shocked him. This was such a wrong time for them. Though she never could have come into his life at a right time, Jed reminded himself, because the chasms between them, if really confronted, would prove to be much too wide to bridge.

She said suddenly, "Jed, why don't you trek over to my place? I can probably rustle us up something better than canned soup."

Cathy could give him a piece of broiled leather and, coming from her, it would taste like ambrosia, Jed thought. But what he needed from her wasn't food. And he couldn't have what he needed from her. He felt as if his common sense were ringing bells, warning that for Cathy and him to become involved *that* way could only lead to disaster.

But Jed climbed into his pickup and followed Cathy's car out onto Lewis Bay Road, all the while trying to talk sense into himself during the brief drive from the hospital to her house.

Cathy was already out of her car by the time he pulled up in the driveway, and Jed saw that she was looking up at Gladys's apartment over the garage.

"I think Gladys's cribbage tournament is going to go on forever," she said.

Cathy had lectured herself all the way back from the hospital, and she was fully aware of the idiocy of having invited Jed to come home with her.

She'd hoped that Gladys would be around. She had planned to use the good sense with which she'd been endowed and promptly invite Gladys to come down and share supper, or a glass of wine, or just some conversation.

Now she felt trapped, and she had to admit that she'd trapped herself.

She sensed that Jed was just as uncomfortable and unsure of the situation as she was, but that didn't help. One of them needed to be in control, but both of them were faltering.

It would be much too easy to fall into each other's arms. And, if that were to happen, they could really tangle up this web they had to share for as long as she was Jed's attorney....

Once inside the house, Cathy gave Jed a can of cold beer and poured a glass of wine for herself. Then she tried to concentrate on pulling a variety of leftovers out of the fridge and studying them. She was good at concocting exotic dishes out of leftovers. She could spice up chunks of meat and vegetables with a liberal dose of curry powder, boil some rice, and she still had half a jar of mango chutney....

She heard music, and came close to toppling over an emotional edge.

Jed had put an old Johnny Mathis cassette on the tape deck. The song lyrics spoke eloquently of love.

Soft lights, sweet music and Jed Moriarty.

The combination was lethal.

When Jed came up behind her and put his arms around her, Cathy instinctively leaned back against the solid warmth of him. His lips nuzzled her neck, moved to the hollow behind her ears. She felt the sensuous probe of his tongue.

Desire spiraled, sharp and hot. Cathy turned within the circle of his arms, reaching for him, pulling his head closer to her level. She nibbled his chin, caught the lower edge of his lip between her teeth, then felt the convulsive intake of his breath.

She tilted her head back and let herself feast on his face, and she saw that his eyes were closed. His eyelashes were gorgeous. God, *he* was gorgeous. She felt the heavy throb of his heartbeat against her chest and, much lower, the male hardness that telegraphed exactly what she was doing to him.

The logic that had been such a part of her for so many years shredded into confetti. What she felt was raw and primitive, intoxicating and overpowering. She would not have believed that her body and her heart could take over her mind like this. For once in her life, Cathy thought hazily, she was all woman. And the atoms of which she was formed, the atoms that made her a woman, were spinning out of control....

Jed opened his eyes. Cathy slipped into a blue sea and was burned by blue fire. She twisted in his embrace, way beyond even making an attempt to analyze what was happening. She and Jed were speaking on a different plane, using a kind of communication that reached a pinnacle of eloquence as Jed played his hands over her body as if she were an exquisite instrument and he a master performer.

He molded her face and then her shoulders with slow, even strokes and, as her flesh tingled in response, he tugged her sweater over her head, then cupped his fingers over the thin blue satin of her bra. She felt her nipples strain against the fabric, and she moaned impatiently. Jed laughed, and said gently, "Easy, sweetheart. It's best when you take it a small step at a time."

Cathy wasn't sure she could take it a small step at a time. Right now, she wanted quantum leaps. She felt

as warm and fluid as molasses, her body heavy with
desire for him. When he slipped off her bra and
rubbed a palm against first one taut nipple and then
the other, she clenched her teeth to keep from crying
out. When his lips followed in the wake of his hands,
she writhed and heard him chuckle.

God, was the man made of steel?

His body answered her, regardless of the restraint he
was showing. And Cathy discovered that her hands
were beginning to move as if they'd been given lives of
their own. She unbuttoned Jed's shirt and fingered the
firmness of his chest, tangled with black hair that was
even curlier than the hair on his head. She pressed his
tight, disciplined muscles, then moved to clasp the
narrow leanness of his waist. Then, slowly, her fingers moved lower and lower. And Jed moaned....

He swept Cathy into his arms so fast that it seemed
only a second before they were up the stairs and into
her bedroom. He laid her down on her bed, and only
then did he pause, and she saw his eyes darken as they
caressed every inch of her.

He was ragged with desire, she could see that. But
even then he hadn't lost the last vestige of control.

He asked huskily, "Are you sure?"

She held out her arms to him.

Cathy felt as if they were moving in a dream as they
undressed each other. Then he knelt over her, and she
saw...all of him. And she felt that there could not
possibly be a more magnificent man in the entire
world.

He was big, he was strong, he was wonderful, and
his passion electrified her. Yet his big hands were re-
markably tender as he introduced her to the miracle of
making love. He was gentle as he touched her, coaxed

her and let his fingers dwell where they gave the greatest pleasure. Then Cathy surprised both of them with the heat of her response. As he kissed her, the control she had kept existed no more.

Jed held her, and let her passion flame; in the aftermath of her first ecstasy she realized how he'd been holding back for her sake.

He was trembling, and for a brief and frightening second, Cathy wondered if she could possibly give him as much as he had just given her. But soon she knew that her first journey had been only a beginning. When Jed entered her, they went into a new dimension, entwined in body, mind, and spirit....

Finally they collapsed, then lay side by side, their hands clinging. Cathy nestled against Jed and pillowed her head on his shoulder, a new and infinitely sweet exhaustion possessing her. And she drifted into sleep before she could tell him that she felt they'd just traveled far beyond the stars he loved so much.

It was still dark when Cathy woke up, to discover that she was alone. The luminous dial on her bedside clock stood at three-thirty and, as the numbers registered, she felt bereft.

At an early hour, while she'd still slept, Jed had left her, and she wondered why. Hadn't he realized when he went that he was taking part of her with him?

She doubted she could ever feel whole again without him.

She looked for a note, but he hadn't left one. She searched for a sign, any sign, that he had been there in her house with her. There was nothing.

She would have questioned her own memory, except that she knew there was no way she could have imagined what had happened between the two of them last night.

Cathy couldn't get back to sleep. At six, she put on sweats and sneakers and drove the few miles to Craigville Beach. There, on the long stretch of sand, she ran along the hard-packed sand, moving at a furious pace.

Why had Jed abandoned her like that?

The thought kept going through her mind. By the time she showered, dressed and left for work, she felt like an empty shell.

It was still early. There was no one else in the office. Gladys wouldn't be along for at least another half hour.

Cathy tried to concentrate on work that needed to be done, but today the law was dry as dust.

Finally she couldn't stand it any longer, and she looked up Jed's number and dialed it.

She hoped she'd have the satisfaction of waking him up, and that maybe he'd spent the balance of his night having bad dreams.

He answered on the second ring. "Moriarty." His tone was clipped; he sounded impatient.

Cathy hadn't thought about what she might say to him. Unprepared, she blurted impulsively, "Why did you leave?"

"Cathy?" He sounded surprised.

"Why did you walk out, Jed?"

"I felt I should clear out before daylight. I realized Gladys would see my truck if I hung around, and I thought you might not like that."

Cathy said resentfully, "Gladys Schwartz is not my keeper."

"I know that. I just thought—"

"You make me feel as if I should be ashamed."

"Ashamed?" he echoed. "God, no. Certainly neither of us has anything to feel ashamed about." He hesitated. "Cathy, I was only thinking of you—"

"My reputation?" she asked coldly.

"Well, yes . . . I guess so."

"I am thirty-seven years old," Cathy said deliberately. He might as well know she was a couple of years older than he was, she thought defiantly. "I think I should be allowed to feel free to lead my own life."

Why, Jed wondered, was Cathy so bent out of shape? Couldn't she give some thought to *him,* and how difficult it had been to leave her bed and sneak out of her house in the darkness?

Sneak.

The word hit him. He *had* sneaked out of her house, and sneaking wasn't his style. But, dammit, he'd done it for her.

Maybe she thought that was old-fashioned of him. Maybe she felt he'd been operating by a code of ethics that was way out of date. He reminded himself that Catherine Merrill was a successful attorney, not a vulnerable female who needed protection.

Protection.

The word hit him.

He began cautiously, "Cathy..."

"Yes?" She still sounded annoyed.

"About last night—"

Jed paused, wondering just how to put this to her without irritating her even more.

"I—er—I hope you were protected," he said finally, unable to think of any way to be more discreet.

Silence could be loud, he discovered. Right now the silence between Cathy and himself beat against Jed's eardrums.

She said flatly, "I don't sleep around, Jed."

"What?"

"I am not on the Pill, if that's what you are asking, because I don't believe in taking any kind of medication needlessly," she informed him.

Before he could either comment or protest, she added icily, "Anyway, don't worry. It's the wrong time of the month."

Chapter Eight

Jed tried to take advantage of the good weather the next couple of days, and he put in long hours of work. But one thing after another went wrong, from banging his thumb with a hammer to running over some broken glass with the pickup and having to buy a new tire.

Having Cathy on his mind—as she was constantly—was impairing his efficiency.

He nearly dialed her number a dozen times, but each time he was halted by the memory of her last comment. There had been such contempt in her voice....

By Friday evening, Jed was so fed up with his own company that he decided to go visit someone who was in worse shape than he was. But as he walked into Bill Grant's hospital room, he wondered about that.

Beth Grant was bidding Bill good-night.

Jed watched them, and envy twinged.

After Beth left, Jed slid onto the chair next to Bill's bed, then looked up to meet Bill's amused hazel eyes.

"Would that I were psychic," Bill drawled. "Then I could read your mind."

Jed shrugged. "There's nothing to read."

Bill grinned. "I imagine Cathy would say the same thing."

"You've seen her?"

"She stopped by for a while late this afternoon. She brought along her file on you."

"*My* file?"

"That's right. She wanted to go over a couple of things. I hope that's okay."

"Why wouldn't it be? You're my lawyer, after all."

"No," Bill corrected, "you have two lawyers in your camp now, but Cathy's the active one. Jed, I think you should realize that she's an extremely competent attorney."

"I never doubted that."

"Cathy feels there may be viable alternatives to your filing Chapter 11," Bill said.

Hearing that made Jed feel strange. He couldn't help but think that Cathy's sense of duty was forcing her to continue with him professionally, even though he was afraid she wanted to write him off personally.

He'd reflected again and again on her reaction to the way he'd slipped out of the house the other night, and wished that he'd thought about leaving some token behind as a remembrance. Hell, he could have gone and picked a flower in her backyard and laid it on the pillowcase. Any kind of gesture that showed he had some sensitivity would have made so much difference.

Instead, the next time he talked to her, he'd brought up the subject of protection in a way that he could now see must have seemed crude to her. But he'd spoken only out of concern for her. God knows he'd been thinking only of her all along, certainly not of himself....

Bill asked patiently, "Did you hear what I just said, Jed?"

Jed nodded. "Yes. And I hope Cathy's right about alternatives. You know I don't want to file Chapter 11 if there's any other way to go."

"When's your next appointment with Cathy?"

"I don't have one."

Bill's eyes narrowed. "Would you mind if I ask what's going on between the two of you? Tell me it's none of my business, if you want to, but I care about Cathy. She's seemed upset lately. When she came in here today, she looked like she hadn't slept in God knows when. Maybe that doesn't have anything to do with you, but... I wonder."

Bill added, "I have the impression Cathy wants to move on your case as fast as she can."

Jed's mouth tightened. "Get it over with, you mean?"

"Possibly. Though I'll tell you one thing—she'll never shortchange you."

"I never thought that, either."

Jed stared at his hands, absorbing the message Bill Grant was giving him.

The other night he and Cathy had shared an experience that had rocked them both. Certainly he would never forget it, just as he would never forget her.

Finally, Bill said, "You haven't answered me."

"Ask again, will you please?" Jed requested.

"What is it with you and Cathy?"

"Bill . . . Cathy should never have taken my case in the first place."

"It's a little late to get into that now, isn't it?"

"Maybe, maybe not. She offered me an out in the beginning. I should have taken it. Maybe I still should take it."

"I suppose you're talking about moving over to another law firm." Bill looked disgusted. "Be sensible, Moriarty. Regardless of the way the two of you feel about each other, it's past the time when it might make sense for you to go to someone else. Cathy's done too much work on your case to do anything like that at this point. It would be a real injustice to her."

Bill looked grim as he went on. "Cathy was only trying to be fair when she offered to give you the names of some other attorneys, because she knew you weren't all that crazy about having her represent you. That's the way she is. Eminently fair. Too much so sometimes, maybe, for her own good.

"People don't give Cathy too many breaks—they don't think she needs them. But she's as human as the next person, and she deserves a lot more out of life than she's getting. She should be married, she should have kids. I've never in my life seen a woman who's crazier about babies."

Bill hesitated, then said, "I'll tell you something in confidence. Beth is two months pregnant, and we're both stalling about telling Cathy. It isn't that she won't be happy for us. She'll be ecstatic. But that's an experience she should be having, too. The problem is, Cathy's given so much to her career, she hasn't kept enough for herself. Which isn't right."

Jed shifted uneasily in his chair as so much came to light. Suddenly he pictured Cathy carrying his child. It was a dizzying concept.

He became aware that Bill Grant was watching him very closely.

"Go easy on her, Jed."

By late Friday afternoon, Cathy admitted that she'd been a bear in the office most of the week. She apologized to Everett as well as to Gladys, but that didn't do much to alter her lousy mood.

She'd skipped lunch to put in time on Jed's file. She'd sandwiched additional work on his case in between appointments. She'd stopped by to see Bill, and had discussed Jed's problem with him. Then she'd gone back to her office, deciding to put in a couple of hours dictating letters to Jed's creditors that could be processed and mailed out Monday.

It was late when she stopped and admitted to herself that life played bizarre tricks. She sat back in her chair and fingered her gold pen. She and Jed were so entirely wrong for each other. He was younger than she was, though by only a couple of years, he was a widower, he was not a professional and they came from entirely different backgrounds.

She thought of the description of Mr. Perfect she'd given Gladys as she rubbed the little Aladdin's lamp on her birthday. And the irony of the difference between fantasy and reality might have been funny, if it weren't so painful.

Cathy tapped her pen against the desk blotter, and the sound echoed through the empty office. Hearing it, she felt so...alone. Tomorrow was Saturday and the weekend stretched ahead; before they left, she'd told Gladys and Everett that come hell or high water, the three of them were going to take this weekend off.

"We'll be burned out if we don't get away from this place for a couple of days," she had stated, and Everett actually had smiled.

Now the thought of a weekend without work seemed . . . abysmal.

Cathy picked up the phone and dialed her father's Cambridge number. She could do with a dose of the city, she thought, as she listened to the phone ring at the other end of the line. Something exciting had to be going on in Boston. Maybe she and the judge could get tickets to a play on Saturday night, and then on Sunday. . .

"*¿Bueno?*" Eduardo said politely.

"Eduardo, is the judge around?" she asked.

"*¿Qué tal, señorita?*" Eduardo responded enthusiastically, and went into a spate of rapid Spanish, which translated into the news that the judge had gone to Maine for the weekend to close up his camp for the season.

That did it.

Cathy gave the office a last check, turned out the lights and let herself out the staff door, determined that she'd find some interesting things to do this weekend even if she had to invent them.

She was almost at her car when she saw the red pickup truck parked right next to it.

Jed Moriarty got out of the cab and came toward her.

Cathy told herself that if she had any spirit she'd get in her car, slam the door and zoom out of the parking lot.

Her feet felt as though they'd been cemented to the asphalt.

Jed loomed over her. The floodlights around the lot slanted across his face so that his features were part light, part shadow.

"We have to talk," he said.

Hadn't she heard that before?

"Jed, this has been a long, rough day. I'm really done in. Another time, maybe, but not now."

"There's no point putting it off, Cathy. And there isn't all that much to say."

That surprised her. "Isn't there?"

"No. There's only one thing I need to make you understand, and I certainly didn't do a very good job of it over the phone. I'll say it again—the only reason I left your house like I did was because I thought it might embarrass you if Gladys knew I'd spent the night with you."

He held up a hand as she started to speak. "Just hold on for a minute, will you, please? Maybe you don't agree, but I was thinking only of you and, dammit, that does make a difference. I *honor* you. That should mean something to you."

No one had ever said anything like that to her before.

"As for anything else," Jed went on doggedly, "I certainly didn't mean to imply that I thought you were sleeping around when I assumed maybe you were on the Pill. I didn't intend anything negative by what I said. I just wanted to be sure you were safe...for your sake, not mine."

"Jed—" Cathy began, but he cut her off.

"One more thing," he said. "I've talked to Bill, and he thinks I'm crazy. But I'm firing you, Cathy."

Cathy stared at him, dazed. Then she croaked, "What did you say?"

"I'm firing you," Jed repeated. "You're off my case. I knew from the beginning that you shouldn't be on it, and I was right. There's no reason why you should be saddled with my problem. So you're off the hook."

Jed turned toward his pickup. But he had one last word to say. "Forget about returning the retainer. I'm sure you've done far more than fifteen hundred dollars' worth of work for me anyway. And . . . I appreciate it."

He got into the pickup, and before Cathy could react, he fired the engine and roared out of the parking lot.

Saturday dawned, bright and beautiful. The sun was reasonably high in the morning sky when Cathy drove to Cedarville, determined to confront Jed.

He had taken a brief midmorning coffee break and was coming out of his trailer when her car ground to a stop almost at his feet.

She was the last person in the world he'd expected to see, and he couldn't avoid the deep ache that swept clear to his bones.

She was wearing jeans and a sweater. He wasn't sure whether the sweater was blue or purple. But whatever color it was, it looked terrific on her.

She grinned and said, "Hi," as if she made it a regular habit to drop by his place.

"Hello," Jed said, surprised that he could speak at all.

Cathy got out of the car. "I thought it was about time I checked out your development."

Jed wondered if he looked as awkward as he felt. "Sure," he agreed lamely.

"Am I interrupting your work?"

"Not really. I can't do much more on the house until the electricians come in."

He watched her gaze wander, and tried to see his property through her eyes. She wasn't seeing the best of Cranberry Estates from here. The choicest lots were around the freshwater pond at the center of the development. But from where they stood, it was still lovely. His trailer was parked in a clearing of woods that were a mix of pine and oak. On this October day, caressed by golden sunlight and fanned by a cool, salty breeze, the pines smelled like Christmas.

"I'll drive you around, if you like," Jed offered.

Cathy smiled at him, and Jed could feel his backbone wobble.

"I'd like," she said.

Jed tried to keep things in proper perspective as he drove her through his acreage. He kept reminding himself that Cathy was here as his attorney—there was nothing personal about this visit. But having her so close was tantalizing beyond belief. She had her hair pulled back in a ponytail, she was wearing very little makeup, she looked incredibly young and so absolutely lovely....

Jed tried to concentrate on detailing his plans for the development to her. He told her about the kind of houses he'd wanted to build on the choice lots around the pond, and then he gave her a guided tour of the house under construction, warning her to watch where she walked and catching her arm a couple of times when she wasn't careful enough and stumbled.

His touch made Cathy willing to fall on her face, if only to have him pick her up. She couldn't believe how much she wanted to be in his arms again, to feel his strength and closeness.

The sun had edged past the zenith by the time they got back to the trailer. Jed expected Cathy to say goodbye and take off.

She fooled him. "Could you take time out for some lunch?" she asked. "Isn't there a place around here where we could get a hamburger or something?"

"Yeah, in the village," Jed admitted, but then he hesitated. Ordinarily, he wouldn't have thought anything of going over to the coffee shop in work clothes. But Cathy deserved better than that.

"I'd have to change," he told her.

"You look okay."

She had to smile at the expression of doubt on his face. "Okay," she thought, was the understatement of the year.

Suddenly, to her surprise, she felt shy. "That's all right," she told him, backing off a little. "I'd probably better run along."

Jed gave her one of his heart-stopping smiles. "Would you as soon settle for a peanut butter and jelly sandwich?"

Cathy sat at a little table that pulled out from the wall in Jed's compact trailer, and marveled at his efficient use of space.

Jed was pretty efficient, too, as he put together their sandwiches. But when she noticed that his left thumb was wrapped in a large Band-Aid, she frowned. "What happened?"

"I whacked myself with a hammer."

He sat down, barely fitting into the space he'd allowed himself. He was trying to keep a discreet distance from Cathy; it was difficult in such close quarters.

As they ate, Cathy tried to look around the little trailer without being too obvious. This was where Jed lived. As far as she knew, just about everything he owned was right here.

Her eyes lingered on his few personal possessions. She saw a glass telephone insulator that was a beautiful shade of turquoise, and she wondered whether or not that was a color he perceived correctly. A carved wooden duck decoy was perched on a windowsill. There were no photographs in evidence, but there were two shelves filled with books. The books appeared to be classics; they were leather-bound and gold-tooled.

Jed, watching her, said, "I found those at a flea market. I got them for just about nothing. *David Copperfield* and *Ivanhoe* and some of Hemingway and some of Goethe and some of Proust."

"Quite a variety," Cathy observed.

"Yes. I've never read as much as I'd like to. Now I'm usually too bushed at night to keep my eyes open. But there'll come a day..."

He offered to make Cathy another sandwich. She declined, and began to fidget with her paper napkin. The atmosphere between them had become casual, friendly. She hated to ruin it.

She said quietly, "You can't fire me, Jed."

For just a second, Jed looked at her with his heart in his eyes. "I already have fired you."

"No," Cathy said. "I can't accept that. I've worked too hard on your case to call a halt on it now. Ask Bill.

We've consulted about what should be done—he agrees that I am taking the right course."

"Cathy...we can't go on together."

Cathy tried to appeal to his reason. "It would be a costly error to start in all over again with a new attorney at this point, Jed."

He avoided her eyes. "Then it's an error I'll have to make."

"Why?" she demanded.

"You know why. I know why."

"I can't accept that," Cathy heard herself say, and couldn't credit her own ears. She couldn't believe that she was pleading like this with a client—even with Jed.

"I'm afraid you'll have to accept it." Jed's eyes were still fixed on the opposite wall.

"Then," Cathy said, "I will institute a suit for breach of contract."

Jed turned to look at her. "Cathy, come on," he protested.

"I'm serious. I refuse to give up your case without a fight. Ask Bill. He'll agree that I'm right."

"You think Bill will say you should sue me for breach of contract?"

"Ask him."

Jed stared at her, and wondered just what in hell he was going to do about her. Couldn't she see that he was trying his damnedest to set her free?

Cathy said, "As I'm sure Bill has told you, I think we have a good chance of avoiding Chapter 11. I believe we can convince the authorities and your insurance company that you have been the victim of vandalism, and that you've had absolutely nothing to do with anything that has happened here.

"The first of the week, I plan to meet with Don Crandon, who is the private investigator working for your insurance company. Bill spoke to him before his accident. He says Crandon is reasonable, and he'll listen to what we have to say. I want you to tell him everything about these latest incidents, down to the most trivial detail—"

"Cathy—"

"Hear me out," Cathy insisted. "If we can put our points across, I think your creditors can be persuaded to stave off action long enough so that you'll have a chance to finish the house you're working on and, hopefully, sell it before winter. Maybe the insurance company won't loosen up funds immediately, but if we can get Crandon on our side, we'll be on our way there, too. I'm not saying that any of this will be easy. But I think we can put it over."

"Why are you doing this?" Jed demanded.

Cathy told him half of the truth. "Because you are my client," she said, "and I intend to represent you to the best of my ability."

And because I've fallen in love with you, she added silently.

Before Jed could probe further, she switched the subject. "What about the vandalism? Have there been any further attempts."

"No," Jed admitted. "But I've been keeping the floodlights on all night."

"Do that. And, Jed..."

"Yes?"

"Please...if you see or hear *anything,* call the cops, will you?"

He nodded. "Yes. I realize you're right about that."

"Good. Now... I'd better get back to Hyannis."

Jed went out to Cathy's car with her. He opened the door for her, then kept his hands glued to his sides. He knew that if he touched her right now, he might not be able to let her go.

At the last instant, she held out a long, cream-colored envelope. Jed saw that the name of her law firm was printed in the upper left-hand corner. But she took off before he could tear the envelope open.

He pulled out a sheet of paper, and read the hand-written message.

You have an appointment with me at four o'clock next Tuesday afternoon.

My charge for broken appointments is five thousand dollars per minute of allotted time—I've put you down for thirty minutes.

A grin crossed Jed's face, and he couldn't push back the bolt of joy that rocketed through him.

His beautiful attorney was incorrigible. But, God, how he loved her!

Chapter Nine

The telephone was ringing and ringing and ringing....

Cathy sat bolt upright in bed, blinking sleep out of her eyes as she stared at the dial on the bedside clock.

Three o'clock in the morning!

Fear swamped her like a cold tidal wave, and she muttered, "Ohmigod, something's happened to the judge."

She grabbed the receiver, and expected to hear Eduardo's voice.

Instead, she heard Gladys ask, "Cathy?"

Cathy's fear intensified. Eduardo had called Gladys first, she decided, so Gladys could break the terrible news....

That was ridiculous. Eduardo didn't even know Gladys's name.

Before Cathy could form a question, Gladys said, "Jed's been hurt."

Cathy leaned back against the pillows, fighting the black terror that seized her.

Her ears felt hollow; Gladys's voice sounded miles away. "They just called from the emergency room at Cape Cod Hospital. Throw on some clothes and I'll be out at my car in five minutes."

Cathy was waiting when Gladys came down the stairs from her apartment.

As they started out of the driveway, Cathy asked tersely, "Do you know what happened?"

"Evidently, there was an explosion in his trailer. I don't have any details."

Cathy closed her eyes and fought a wave of dizziness. *An explosion!* She trembled as she visualized the worst possible scenario.

"Did Jed ask the hospital to call you?"

"No. Apparently he was unconscious when they took him in, and someone found one of the firm's envelopes in his pocket."

The envelope she'd given him with that ridiculous message.

Gladys said, "The cops went around to the office and talked to the night watchman. Since I'm the office manager, he has my number in case of emergencies. He gave it to the cops, they gave it to the people in the ER and they took it from there."

When they reached the hospital, the lights in the waiting room were dim, the atmosphere hushed. There was none of the bustle of daytime activity, and the quiet seemed ominous to Cathy. Only serious cases were rushed to emergency rooms in the small hours of the morning, she warned herself. Her chest muscles constricted.

Jed was in a small cubicle, lying on an examining table. His legs were so long that his feet came close to hanging over the end.

Cathy moved toward him cautiously, and saw that his eyes were closed. Those long, dark lashes fanned the rims of his cheekbones. There was a patch of bandage on his forehead, and it looked like a couple of locks of his dark, curly hair had been singed. Fluid dripped into his arm from a liquid-filled plastic bag. Cathy looked away from the intravenous equipment, and focused on his hands. They were heavily bandaged.

When she saw his chest rise and fall, she gave a silent prayer of thanks. Then she turned as the nurse who had followed her into the cubicle said gently, "Mr. Moriarty, Ms. Merrill is here."

Jed's eyes flew open. They looked bluer and darker then rare sapphires, and they smoldered.

"What the hell are you doing here?" he demanded hoarsely.

Cathy was so stunned, she couldn't speak.

She saw him close his eyes again, saw his throat muscles work and a spasm of pain cross his face. Her heart went out to him, but she also was going through her own kind of agony. Never before in her life had she felt more helpless.

She tentatively touched the blanket that covered Jed, swallowing hard. She wanted so desperately to help him, to do everything for him. She wanted to care for him, to keep him from hurting....

He grated, "Get out of here, will you?"

Cathy's insides twisted. Didn't he have any idea what he was doing to her?

She studied his face. His rigid features were etched with stubborn pride, a pride that transcended pain.

Well, she thought defiantly, Jed needed her, and she was not going to let him push her away from him. She would not allow him to shut her off.

She asked softly, "Can you talk, Jed?"

That brought a response. He opened his eyes again, and blue fire scorched her. "What do you think I was just doing?"

"Can you tell me what happened?"

"No. I talked to the cops. That's enough."

"Are you going to be admitted?"

"You mean are they going to hole me up in here? Hell, no. I told the nurse to call a cab for me."

"You're saying you plan to go back to the trailer?"

He said grimly, "I doubt there's any trailer to go back to."

Cathy shuddered.

"There's a little motel over in Cedarville, not far from Cranberry Estates," Jed said. "I'm going there. It'll do for tonight."

"It isn't night anymore, Jed. It's after three o'clock in the morning."

"So I lost a couple of hours someplace. Look, Cathy, I'm okay. I'll be okay. You said it's after 3:00 a.m.?" He frowned. "You shouldn't be here."

"Gladys is out in the waiting room. And, Jed . . . I don't think the hospital will release you unless you leave here with someone who can take care of you."

His glance was scathing. "I'm not a kid, Cathy, and I'm not an idiot. I can take care of myself."

She had to say it. "Not with those hands, you can't."

Jed looked at the bandages, then glanced away, refusing to meet her eyes.

"I'll manage," he muttered.

The nurse had left Cathy with Jed, but now she came back into the cubicle.

"Dr. Phelps wants you to rest another half hour or so, Mr. Moriarty," she told Jed. "That will give us time to get your paperwork together. The doctor will be writing some instructions and orders for some medication. He'll give everything to Mrs. Schwartz. He planned to admit you, but he's agreeable to your going home with Mrs. Schwartz and Ms. Merrill, as Mrs. Schwartz suggested." The nurse gave Jed a cheery smile. "It won't be much longer."

Jed waited until he was sure the nurse had left, then he swore volubly.

Cathy had to smile. When he'd finally quieted down, she said, "Looks like you're caught between a rock and a hard place, doesn't it, Moriarty? Which is it to be? The hospital? Or Gladys and me?"

She saw Jed's blue eyes glisten, and she was staggered.

Jed Moriarty with tears in his eyes?

He blinked, and murmured, "There's no reason why you should do this."

She put it to him. "If our positions were reversed, wouldn't you do it for me?"

"Yeah, but that's different."

He sighed deeply. "I know I must come on like an ungrateful bastard," he admitted. "It's just that I...I'm not used to having to depend on anyone else."

Cathy's emotions were getting to her, and it was hard to keep her voice level. "We all need help sometimes, Jed. We all need someone we can turn to and depend upon."

"Maybe. But there's no reason why it should be you, Cathy."

"There's no reason why it shouldn't be." Her voice so low he could barely hear her, Cathy added, "I care about you."

The medication Jed had been given to dull his pain was taking effect, though his hands hurt like hell. But though he was slightly groggy, Cathy's words filtered through to him.

I care about you.

He was silently repeating the four words over and over when he dozed off.

When he woke up, he knew a moment of panic. The small white cubicle was empty. She had left. Cathy had gotten fed up with his miserable attitude and she'd walked out on him.

It served him damn well right.

Jed tried to sit up, and had to lie back down again. His head fell like a misshapen watermelon, too heavy, too awkward to manage. After a minute, he made another attempt, and this time he levered himself to a sitting position. It took another try to push his legs over the edge of the examining table.

His bandaged hands made doing anything at all incredibly difficult. He looked at the big, painful white clumps, and groaned. He had no idea how bad the burns were . . . and he made his living with his hands.

What more could happen to send everything he'd worked and planned for straight down the tube?

The nurse—who'd really been very good to him—came into the cubicle and chided, "What are you doing sitting up like that? You should have pushed the bell."

Cathy appeared just behind her.

Jed met Cathy's anxious brown velvet gaze across the space that stretched between them. She looked so beautiful to him, she took his breath away.

She grinned, and said, "Looks like they're ready to spring you."

"I'll get a wheelchair," the nurse said.

"I'll walk," Jed immediately insisted.

Cathy shook her head. "No way. This time, like it or not, you're going to ride, Moriarty."

Cathy wanted to ask Jed a thousand questions, but she knew they'd have to wait.

The first order of business, after she and Gladys helped him into her house, was to get him up the stairs and into the bed in her guest room.

He tried to cooperate, but he was exhausted. Undressing him was quite a job; right now he was mostly dead weight. Gladys got his shirt off, and his shoes and socks, but when she reached for the zipper on his denims, he protested.

"Come on, Jed," Gladys teased, "I have a son as old as you are. I'm not assaulting your manhood."

Jed grunted, but let Gladys slide the dense material over his hips.

He was left wearing a pair of snug white briefs, and though this was certainly no moment for passion, Cathy couldn't evade the surge of desire that welled up in her. Her craving was hot and sweet, filled with love as well as need. She bent and tenderly pulled the bedcovers over Jed, then brushed his forehead with her lips; she was thankful that Gladys, who was neatly folding up Jed's clothes, was too preoccupied to notice.

They left a night-light on in the bedroom, then went downstairs. Gladys brewed herb tea, and it wasn't until they'd taken the tea into the living room that Gladys said solemnly, "He was lucky."

"You found out something more?" Cathy asked quickly.

Gladys nodded. "Some. I talked to one of the EMTs on the Cedarville Rescue Squad. He was still at the hospital. He said it's a miracle Jed wasn't killed."

Cathy's hand was shaking so that she couldn't hold her teacup. She set it aside. "Did he know what happened?"

"He said from what he heard, it seems that some kind of an incendiary device was tossed through the window in Jed's trailer and blew up...just about everything. Somehow Jed escaped."

"Gladys, did someone see the explosion?"

"I don't know," Gladys admitted. "Obviously someone must have, or the police wouldn't have been called."

"I suppose so. But..."

"What are you getting at, Cathy?"

"I went over to Cedarville yesterday, and I saw Jed's trailer. It's in the middle of a lot of woods—there's nothing around. The whole development is pretty isolated, for that matter."

"Maybe there was a motorist driving along a road nearby, and he saw the flare...."

"Maybe."

Cathy sank back against the sofa pillows. Gladys was worried as she looked at her. Cathy was paler than Jed was, and she seemed just as exhausted.

"Gladys..." Cathy was having trouble with this question. "Did the EMT say anything about Jed's hands? Did he give you any idea of how bad the burns might be?"

"Not the EMT, no. But I did talk to the emergency room physician who took care of Jed. He wasn't making any judgment about the burns. Jed has an appointment at the hospital tomorrow morning so his hands can be examined and the bandages changed. But it does seem that there's one thing for sure. He won't be doing any building for quite a while."

How was Jed going to take that?

Gladys said, "Don't look so stricken, dear. This isn't the end of the world. Let's be thankful that Jed's alive and has youth and excellent health on his side. My guess is that he'll be a very quick healer."

Cathy said slowly, "He still isn't safe."

Gladys was perplexed. "What do you mean?"

"Someone hates him, Gladys. Maybe at first whoever it is just wanted to see him fail, go broke. They torched his two spec houses last summer. There have been incidents of vandalism all along. But this attack tonight was personal. Whoever it is planned to *kill* Jed this time."

Her mind went into overdrive. "I'll need to talk to the Cedarville police myself, and the people from the fire department and rescue squad who responded to the call to Jed's place. And I'll want to see the insurance company's private investigator as soon as I can." She searched her memory for his name, and found it. "Don Crandon. And Bill—"

"Take a deep breath, Cathy. You don't have to start running a marathon. My bet is that all of those people are going to bend over backward to help you."

"Well, there's one thing for sure. I'm not about to let Jed be persecuted any longer," Cathy announced defiantly.

"What are you talking about?"

"No one's helped Jed up till now, Gladys. Matter of fact, he's been under suspicion of arson—and vandalism, too, I suppose—because of his financial problems. Now I'm going to make sure the people in authority see the other side of the coin."

"Cathy—" Gladys wanted to be sure she chose the right words "—I'm very glad you're on Jed's side, and I'm sure you'll do everything you can for him, both as his attorney and as his friend. But remember that you're also going to have to let Jed handle as much as he can himself. He's the most independent man I've ever met."

Cathy was getting a good taste of that independence by noon that Sunday.

Jed had slept through most of the day, but by afternoon he had insisted on getting up, and somehow managed to handle pulling his clothes on by himself.

Now, as they sat side by side at the kitchen table, he said testily, "Damn it, Cathy, I can feed myself."

Cathy gritted her teeth to keep from saying something she'd be sorry for. Jed was having trouble trying to wield a soup spoon with his bandaged hands, but when she'd suggested she might help him, he'd reared back as if she were a cobra about to strike.

Soup, she decided, had been a lousy idea. But what *could* he eat by himself?

She watched as he determined to manage, and he *did* manage, though slowly and with difficulty . . . and painfully as well.

She broke a roll for him, buttered it and put it on a plate positioned so it was in easy reach.

Jed slammed the soup spoon down on the table. "Maybe I should have checked into the hospital after all," he snarled.

Stung, Cathy demanded, "Will you tell me what it is I'm doing that's annoying you so much?"

"You're acting like you're my mother," Jed snapped. "I had a mother. I don't want another one."

Cathy looked at him as if he'd hit her. She started to push her chair away, and Jed stood and came around the table so fast, she had no chance to move very far.

His arms went around her. He tugged her toward him, using his forearms rather than his hands. He murmured in her ear, "I'm sorry. Honestly, I'm sorry. I'm having a rough time getting used to being so . . . so helpless, that's all. Don't think I don't appreciate what you're doing for me."

Cathy's face was buried against his chest. Her voice was muffled. "You don't have to *appreciate* anything. Just don't be so pigheaded."

Jed's laugh was shaky. "I guess I was born that way. . . ."

He tried to pull her even closer, then gave up. He felt as though he had a big bundle tied at the end of each arm. There was no way he could touch Cathy the way he wanted to. Frustration swept through him, and something more. Fear.

Just how bad were his hands?

Jed stared down at his bandaged hands. They would heal, he knew that, but *how* would they heal? He needed the full use of his fingers—the nerves, the muscles, the tendons. He needed strong hands, and he knew that sometimes people who'd been badly burned were left with little better than twisted claws.

Even if that happened, he'd survive. He wasn't a quitter. But if yesterday the odds had been running high against Cathy Merrill and him ever being what he wished so much they could be to each other, today those odds were a million times worse. Yesterday, he'd had a future with a question mark to offer her. Today, he had nothing.

It was a relief to have Gladys walk into the kitchen.

Jed let go of Cathy, and she moved away from him, but a rosy flush he couldn't help but love stained her cheeks.

Gladys, imperturbable as ever, said, "You made the evening news on TV, Jed. So I think we'd better prepare ourselves for some follow-up interviews."

"I don't want to talk to any reporters," Jed growled.

"I'll second that," Cathy agreed. "I'll take any calls that come for you, and if anyone shows up here at the house—"

"Look, I'm not pushing this problem on *you*," Jed informed her. "I can say 'No comment' over the phone, and I can close the door in someone's face, if I have to."

"Neither one of you has to become involved," Gladys interceded. "I can take care of the press. You might dictate a statement to me, Jed."

"Gladys, I'll be the judge of what Jed should or shouldn't say right now," Cathy put in.

"The hell you will be," Jed retorted. "I appreciate what you're trying to do, Cathy, but give me a little room when it comes to making decisions, okay?"

Cathy bristled. Gladys wisely tried to change the subject.

"Jed's medical appointment is at nine-thirty tomorrow morning," she said. "His doctor is on call then, so he'll be seeing him at the hospital instead of in his office. I thought I might go by our office early, and then cut back here and pick up Jed—"

"Why not postpone my first couple of appointments and I'll take him," Cathy suggested.

"I thought it might be easier the other way around—" Gladys began, but Jed interrupted her.

"Stop fighting over me, ladies," he told them, but his smile was not amused. "I can go by myself. All I have to do is call a cab."

The school principal in Gladys surfaced. "Let's not overcomplicate this." She fixed Jed with her sternest expression. "I'll be by for you at a quarter past nine."

Cathy looked from one to the other, and decided not to get in the middle. She had her own problems with Moriarty, and in comparison, the matter of transportation to Cape Cod Hospital was pretty simple.

Gladys said, "Incidentally, I called Bill, and I was glad I did. He'd seen the TV news and he was worried about Jed. He told me to ask you to check in with him tomorrow."

Cathy nodded. "Yes, I intend to do that."

"Maybe when we're at the hospital we can run up and see Bill for a few minutes . . . if you're up to that, Jed."

Jed agreed. "If you can spare the time, Gladys."

"Gladys can spare it," Cathy said rather shortly. She added, "I thought about making a few phone calls tonight, but Sunday night's not the best time to talk to people. I especially want to try to get hold of Don Crandon in the morning, though—he's the insurance company's investigator. I thought maybe I could persuade him to come over here tomorrow afternoon, and in that case I will need to reschedule some appointments—"

Cathy was thinking out loud, and she stopped short as she saw the irritated expression on Jed's face.

"I know now how kids feel when grown-ups talk about them as if they weren't in the same room," he said, caustically. "I know you want to make plans, Cathy, and I guess I should be used to the way that mind of yours works by now. But I do have excellent hearing and pretty damned good vision, and you don't need to lay everything out as if I'd lost both. I'd like to be consulted, okay?"

Cathy saw Gladys turn away and try to hide a smile. And, as much as Jed could irk her, she nearly smiled herself.

Gladys was right. He did have to be one of the most independent men in the world. And she was beginning to realize that was something she was going to have to learn to live with.

Chapter Ten

"Don't you think you should get back to your office?" Jed suggested.

It was Monday afternoon and he and Cathy were in her living room, each of them sitting in an armchair as if they'd decided by mutual consent to avoid the potential intimacy of the couch.

"No," Cathy said. "Gladys managed to juggle my appointments because my being at the meeting you scheduled with Don Crandon is more important."

Then she added, "I insist, as your attorney, that I am present whenever you confer with *anyone* about *any* of this," Cathy said.

Jed tried again to make her understand his reasoning.

"Look," he said, "it's more than enough that you took the time to come home and fix lunch for me, but there's no need for you to hang around while I talk to

Don Crandon. When he phoned after you'd left for work and said he'd like to come out and talk to me, I saw no reason to refuse him.''

Despite Cathy's belligerent expression, he continued, ''Your representing me has nothing to do with arson, vandalism, accidents, explosions or anything else that's been going down. That's not why I hired you.''

Cathy wanted to throttle him. ''You couldn't be more wrong.'' She bit out each word. ''If we're going to keep you from having to file Chapter 11, it's essential for you to be cleared of all traces of suspicion when it comes to anything that's happened at Cranberry Estates.''

''I think even the cops have admitted the scenario has changed,'' Jed pointed out. ''Only a damned fool could think that I'd not only destroy my own property, but come close to destroying myself, as well.''

He glanced at his hands as he spoke. The doctor who had changed the bandages that morning had not been especially vocal, and Jed had to admit that he hadn't asked too many questions, either.

The doctor had said something about possible skin grafting later; he had mentioned therapy and time for healing. Jed had listened, wishing a few things could be clarified. Maybe it was too early to clarify very much. Maybe even the experts weren't sure yet how his hands were going to heal, especially his left hand, which was the worse of the two. He supposed he could consider himself lucky that he was right-handed.

He could consider himself lucky on two counts, for that matter. His new spec house hadn't been touched in this latest incident, which was a miracle. It, too, could so easily have been sent up in flames.

Bill Grant said as much when Jed and Gladys were allowed to see him for a few minutes before they left the hospital, even though visiting hours had not yet started. Then Gladys insisted that they make a side trip to a men's clothing store so Jed could get a few things he needed badly. When he protested that he didn't have any money with him—and his checkbook had probably been lost in the explosion—she convinced him in her best school principal manner that his credit was good with her.

Gladys left Jed at the house, where he expected to be alone. But he found Cathy in the kitchen, fixing something for his lunch, and the sight of her at the stove almost did him in.

How could he ever pay either Cathy or Gladys for what they were doing for him? he wondered. His heart filled, and his eyes damn near filled, too.

Cathy turned and looked at him standing in the kitchen doorway. She was silent for a moment, then asked, "How did it go?"

"Okay, I guess."

"Come and sit down," she invited. "I think I've solved a problem."

He lifted an eyebrow. "Oh?"

She waved a pair of tongs she usually used for serving spaghetti. "I'm making us grilled cheese sandwiches," she said. "You can use these to pick up the sections. I'm pretty sure you'll be able to manage with them. They should work well with a lot of things."

"Very... inventive," Jed said, but he still made no move toward the kitchen table.

His damned hands made him feel so clumsy. He hated to eat in front of her, but Cathy gave him no choice. After he caved in to her demands and sat down, he discovered she was right—the tongs worked pretty well.

With lunch over, Cathy had tried to get Jed to go upstairs and take a nap. He had wanted to say he'd be glad to, if she'd go with him, but he'd held his tongue. Instead, he'd suggested they go into the living room.

"Now," Cathy went on, "I've talked to the police chief over in Cedarville and the fire chief, who also heads the rescue squad. Someone called in about the explosion, Jed."

Coming out of his reverie, he stared at her. "What are you saying?"

"A man called the police around two o'clock yesterday morning. He said there was trouble at Cranberry Estates. A bad fire, and he thought someone was hurt."

"I don't suppose he identified himself?"

"No."

"Cathy, do you think the caller was the guy who's done all the damage?"

"That's occurred to me, yes. I think maybe he wanted to scare you to death, but maybe he didn't want to kill you." Cathy's voice shook with this last comment.

"That does it. You have to back out of this, Cathy. I don't want my name connected with you."

"Oh, God, Jed." He was driving her crazy. "Let's not start on that tack all over again."

"I'm not being stubborn," Jed said, "I'm being realistic. Believe me. I tried to tell the cops last summer that there had to be a psycho behind *that* fire. Now if the person who tossed whatever the hell it was into my trailer phoned the police himself, that proves my psycho theory, wouldn't you say? Sane people don't do things like that."

Jed stood up and paced restlessly. Suddenly the room seemed much too small to hold him.

"Cathy, if we're dealing with a true psychotic personality we can't take chances," he insisted. "Perhaps the explosion was frightening enough that he backed off. Perhaps *then* he didn't want to be responsible for killing me, and he called the cops thinking maybe someone could get to me in time. But that doesn't mean he won't change his mind and try again. Even worse... if you're linked with me he may try to get at me through you...."

"That's ridiculous, Jed." Cathy tried to sound convincing, but she knew there could be truth in what he said.

"The state police have their arson squad in on this now," she told him. "Cedarville will have plenty of help. The Staties are also going to help the local police patrol Cranberry Estates—they'll be keeping a close watch on things."

"Too close, maybe," Jed mumbled.

"Jed," Cathy warned, "if you're getting the idea again of setting a trap, forget about it."

Jed glanced at his bandaged hands, and said ruefully, "I doubt I'd be much good at trap-setting just now, Cathy."

Private investigators seldom, if ever, became involved in the areas of the law Cathy normally practiced. She had to smile as she thought that her father might not have been surprised by Don Crandon, but she was.

He was an attractive man in his early forties, tall and slender with light brown hair and very light gray eyes. His casual manner, Cathy thought, could be deceptive; she was not about to discount the sharp intelligence she saw in those light eyes. He quietly questioned Jed in a low-key manner and essentially let Jed tell his own story.

"I . . . just wasn't sleepy Saturday night," Jed began, and avoided looking at Cathy. She was the reason he hadn't been able to settle in and go to bed. He kept thinking about her being in his trailer that afternoon, and he marveled at how he'd managed to keep from making love to her.

Thinking about making love to her had evoked its own kind of torture; God, how he'd wanted her, as he sat alone in his trailer with the moon showering shreds of silver through the trees and across the stubby grass in the clearing.

"I was reading," Jed went on. He'd picked out *Anna Karenina* from his collection of classics, and let himself be transported back to the Russia of an earlier age.

"I guess it was sometime after one when this . . . this object crashed through the window back of me. I got out of the way of the shattering glass, and then I saw something that looked like a fireball about the size of a large orange, maybe even a grapefruit.

"My natural impulse was to try to put it out. I grabbed a blanket from the foot of the bed and started beating down on it, thinking I could smother it. But then . . . it exploded. Flames spurted in every direction. . . ."

Jed glanced at his bandages. "I couldn't get my hands out of the way fast enough. They got the brunt of it. Then the fire caught the covers on the bed, and the window curtains. I knew the whole place could go up in seconds, and I had to get out.

"I tried to salvage the plans for my development. I tried to grab papers, records. But the flames were spreading so fast I found myself clutching at floating embers.

"Somehow...I made it outside, and I can remember stumbling toward what I hoped was safety. Then I guess I passed out."

Crandon nodded. "They found you at the edge of the woods. It's lucky the fire didn't catch the trees."

Crandon leaned forward. "We found enough remnants so we can say that the explosive device was a kind of bomb—a homemade contraption, which didn't make it any the less effective."

Jed said, "It's a wonder he didn't toss the same kind of thing into the house I've been building."

"He did plan to set fire to the house," Crandon confided. "We think he gave up when he saw the damage he'd done to the trailer. Evidently he didn't realize just how effective the bomb was going to be, and when he saw what happened, he was afraid you had been killed. We think at that point he fled and headed for a phone and called the police."

"So...there *is* an arsonist." Jed fought back resentment. Why hadn't people listened to him sooner?

Crandon said slowly, "There doesn't seem to be much doubt about that. On the way to the trailer he stopped at the house you're building and left his signature, though that wasn't his intention. If he hadn't changed course, there wouldn't have been much left.

As it is, we found several cans of kerosene stashed in the house, and some flammable material. A couple of old mattresses, dirty, oil-soaked cloths..."

Jed shook his head, disgusted with himself. "I didn't hear a damned thing. It's a fair distance from the house to the trailer, but even so..."

He said, "I should have been a helluva lot more alert. I let down my guard. While I was reading I was playing an old Johnny Mathis tape on my stereo."

Maybe a copy of the same tape he'd played the night they made love?

Cathy met Jed's eyes, and didn't try to hold back what she was feeling. For a moment, his expression was bleak. But then he smiled at her.

Crandon said, "Ms. Merrill has told me about the recent vandalism."

Jed's smile faded.

"She said you've seen a pickup truck around your development a few times."

"That's right."

"Actually, you saw what you think was the same truck before the fire that burned up your two spec houses last summer?"

"Yes."

"You told the Cedarville police about that at the time?"

"Yes. But they didn't pay a great deal of attention to me."

"I didn't pay as much attention to you as I should have, either," Crandon conceded. "This isn't much of an excuse, but we've been up to our necks in arson investigations the past couple of years, and overall they follow pretty much of a pattern. Most of the time we know they've been set by people hoping to collect insurance because they're up a tree financially. But arson is difficult, often impossible, to prove. So, I admit, we get pretty cynical.

"The Cedarville police have an APB out for the pickup," Crandon concluded. "If it's still in the area, we should be able to find it."

He had not been taking notes, but now he produced a microcassette recorder. "If it's okay with you," he told Jed, "I'd like to get some of the things you've told me down for the record."

Cathy sat back, wishing that Jed didn't have to recount his terrible experience again; on the other hand she could see that Crandon, experienced investigator that he was, wanted to hear the details twice.

Maybe Jed still wasn't off the hook where this man was concerned, sympathetic though he seemed to be.

A short while later, Cathy saw Don Crandon to the door, then came back to the living room to see that Jed was leaning over in his chair, his arms akimbo, and he looked as if he were in pain.

She said quickly, "Let me get you a pill."

"No..." He shook his head. "They make me groggy."

She smiled. "You're among friends. The worst that could happen is that you might fall asleep for a while. Would that be so bad?"

He let her help him with the pills, and obediently swallowed some of the water she held out to him. Then Cathy put the water glass aside and pulled a chair close to his.

"I have a gut feeling Crandon's on your side," she said. "But I could be wrong, and we can't afford to take chances. We need to dig up what we can by ourselves."

"What are you talking about, Cathy?" Jed sounded very weary.

"I keep thinking about your brothers-in-law," Cathy admitted. "You told me they blamed you for their father's death. That seems unreasonable."

"I'm glad you think so. I also told you they've gotten over that, Cathy."

"How can you be sure?"

He sighed. "I can't, I suppose. I've often wished I'd gone to Tony and told him the truth, but it would never have done any good. He was so crazy about Angela she could do no wrong in his eyes. So he had to blame me...for the failure of our marriage, for our not having any kids."

"What *was* the truth, Jed?"

"Tony didn't know his daughter. Neither did I, for a long time."

"What do you mean?"

Jed shrugged. "Angela was on the Pill long before I met her. And she never went off it. Angela wasn't about to be saddled down with kids."

Cathy wasn't sure whether the pain she saw on his face stemmed from his injuries, or from his memories of Angela.

She didn't try to find out. She wasn't ready to hear any more revelations, and she doubted Jed was either willing or able to make them.

She stood, bent over and grabbed his wrists above the bandages. She tugged hard, but there was no way she could budge him.

"Come on," Cathy urged. She smiled. "I'm afraid I can't carry you, Moriarty."

Jed saw the smile through a haze that made Cathy look like a beautiful angel. He told himself the medication wasn't *that* powerful but it was dizzying enough to make him imagine that Cathy had gossamer wings, and perched on her bronze hair was a golden crown that tilted ever so slightly.

He let her help him up, and he loved the feel of her smooth palms on his wrists. He was docile as she steered him to the couch, and he made as long a deal as he could out of getting down on it. He decided to put his pride in his pocket for once, and enjoy Cathy's solicitude.

But once Jed was supine, he made a calculated surprise move. Cathy was still holding his wrists, leaning over him, and with a little pressure from him she lost her balance. She tumbled on top of him, and Jed didn't let go.

Her hair, which she'd combed carefully before meeting with Crandon, swept forward to tumble in glorious waves that framed her face. Slightly fuzzy though he was, Jed saw the flush that stained her cheeks so that they looked like rose petals.

He wanted to see if they felt like rose petals, but his bandaged hands wouldn't allow that. Bandaged hands or no bandaged hands, though, he was not about to let go of Cathy. He tugged her toward him, and she protested, "I'll hurt you."

Jed corrected her. "No, sweetheart. You'll heal me."

He held his face up to hers, his lips an invitation Cathy couldn't resist. She kissed him, and the sweet, warm intensity that flowed between them brought tears to her eyes.

Jed murmured, "Just curl up beside me for a little while, will you?"

Cathy wouldn't have believed the couch was wide enough to hold anything more than Jed Moriarty. But it was.

She snuggled next to him, pillowed her head on his shoulder and felt the strength of his arm around her. Just then, nothing else mattered.

After a time, she heard the tenor of Jed's breathing change. She felt the rise and fall of his chest, and she stole a glance at him. Those fantastic dark lashes swept the edges of his cheeks. He looked young, and at peace. A smile curved his lips.

Cathy snuggled against him again and closed her eyes.

A few minutes later, Gladys, having finished her day at the office, came in and saw the two of them, and she succumbed to a wave of sweet sadness. Once, she thought, she'd loved like that. The analogy surprised her.

But then she looked again at Jed and Cathy, and it seemed to her that they were such a perfect pair. From the contrast in their coloring to the contrast in their personalities, they were alive and exciting and God knows they would never be bored with each other any more than she and Sherm ever had been.

Yes, Gladys thought, her boss lady and this client were right for each other. But she was afraid it was going to be hard to convince them of that.

Gladys picked up the little lamp she'd given Cathy on her birthday, rubbed it fervently and made a wish.

Cathy woke up and stared into pitch blackness. She felt a warm body next to her, and it took her a minute to realize this was reality.

Yes, she was here in her own living room. Yes, Jed was lying next to her on her living-room couch. And he still seemed to be fast asleep.

She eased off the couch. He stirred, and she was afraid she had awakened him. But then she heard the even, deep sound of his breathing, and she tiptoed out of the room.

Gladys was in the kitchen, working on a crossword puzzle. She looked up when Cathy came in. "I was wondering if the two of you would sleep straight through till morning."

Cathy glanced at the kitchen clock and thought that there must have been a power outage while she was asleep—well, something, anyway, to put the clock so completely out of sync. It couldn't be almost midnight!

"Why didn't you wake me up?" she moaned.

"There are moments, love, when it's best to let nature take its course. Incidentally, your father has called three times."

"He's back from Maine?"

"Yes. It's almost midnight, as you just observed, and your father got back from Maine several hours ago. Eduardo, I believe his name is, must have told the judge the minute he got in the door that you'd called last Friday. Evidently the judge gave Eduardo hell for not having the Royal Canadian Mounties charge over the border and sound a red alert. Are your phone calls to the judge that rare, Cathy?"

Cathy was not about to answer.

"Anyway," Gladys continued, "by the third call, I was afraid that if the judge kept at it I would drift off before I caught the phone on the first ring, and then it might wake you and Jed. So I filled him in on what's going on.''

"Ouch," Cathy said.

"I'm not sure how to interpret that." Gladys's brow wrinkled. "I have this feeling that perhaps you and the judge don't communicate as well as you might. I think you intimidate each other."

Intimidate the judge? Cathy wanted to laugh, but all of a sudden the thought didn't seem very funny.

"Anyway," Gladys continued, "the judge says that Eduardo will be coming down first thing in the morning to assist you."

"Eduardo?"

Gladys nodded. "Yes, and before you start protesting, let me tell you I told the judge I think that's an excellent idea. I have the feeling that Jed will be a lot more comfortable with Eduardo's ministrations than he will with yours—or mine, for that matter. Also, Eduardo can handle the cooking and cleaning—"

"And I'm supposed to go back to the office and forget that Jed's here with both hands all bandaged up?"

Cathy couldn't hide her bitterness.

Gladys said gently, "No one's about to ask you to do that. Anyway, the judge is going to call you tomorrow morning. He said if he doesn't get you at the office, he'll call here. He wanted to remind you that he's speaking at a dinner here in Hyannis Thursday night, and I believe you're going with him? I think it's something to do with the Barnstable County Bar Association."

"Oh, God," Cathy moaned. "The judge isn't just going to make a speech . . . he's supposed to get some kind of an award. He asked me at least a month ago to go with him. I put it down on my calendar at the office, but I'd forgotten all about it.''

''Well, now you can remember it,'' Gladys said placidly.

She set aside the crossword puzzle. ''I think the next task is to get Jed Moriarty off that couch, persuade him to eat something and then help him get into bed. I have an antibiotic he's supposed to take, and he has to have some food first.''

Gladys started out of the kitchen, then glanced back long enough to say, ''I think by tomorrow morning, boss lady, we'll both be thankful to have Eduardo come aboard.''

Chapter Eleven

"*Señorita*, there is a Señora Smithson on the telephone."

Cathy resented the interruption. She was trying to convince Jed that he shouldn't even think about going over to Cranberry Estates this afternoon to survey the ruins of his trailer, among other things.

She had just said, "Don Crandon will be there, and probably adjustors from the insurance company. The arson squad will still be swarming all over the place. The police will be around, probably a couple of people from the fire marshal's office, as well. You're the last person they need on the scene."

Now she sighed. Eduardo had been in Hyannis for less than three hours, and he was already in charge of the household. Still, she should have told him that when she was with someone, as she was right now with Jed, he should hold phone calls and take messages.

She started to suggest that, but she was too late.

"I told the *señora* you are available," Eduardo said, as he held out the cordless phone. He didn't even have the grace to look chagrined despite the hard stare Cathy leveled at him.

Cathy, using her carefully modulated lawyer's voice, said, "Good morning, Mrs. Smithson."

"Please excuse me for bothering you at home, Ms. Merrill," Genevieve Smithson answered. "Mrs. Schwartz was kind enough to give me your number because I've been so concerned about Jed Moriarty."

"Jed Moriarty?" Cathy echoed.

The subject under discussion perked up his ears.

"I saw the news about the explosion in his development and I've read the newspaper stories," Mrs. Smithson said. "I hope his injuries aren't serious. I tried to reach him at Cape Cod Hospital, but he's not on their patient list."

"Jed Moriarty is doing very well." Cathy faced Jed as she spoke.

"Well, that's a relief," the elderly woman said. "I'd like to contact Mr. Moriarty, Ms. Merrill. I have something to discuss with him I think he might find of interest."

"Wait just a minute, please."

Cathy capped her hand over the phone. "Do you think you can handle this?" she asked Jed.

His eyebrows shot upward. "You're asking me to speak to Mrs. Smithson?"

"Mrs. Smithson," Cathy said by way of an answer, "Mr. Moriarty and I have been in conference here at my house. Let me put him on."

Before Jed could protest, Cathy shoved the receiver toward him. He managed to cup a bandaged hand around the phone.

"Mrs. Smithson?"

Cathy liked his low, mellow voice, and she sat back to enjoy a little eavesdropping.

What could Genevieve Smithson possibly want to consult Jed about? she wondered. She'd spoken to her elderly client a couple of times since their last meeting, and she still hadn't been able to shake her conviction that she should leave her fortune to Sylvester.

Cathy grinned. Maybe Mrs. Smithson wanted Jed to build a unique doghouse for Sylvester, with a yard around it paved with gold bricks.

Mrs. Smithson, Cathy noted, was doing most of the talking. But then Jed said emphatically, "No."

Cathy sat up straighter. She doubted anyone often said no like that to Genevieve Smithson.

Then she heard Jed say, "I don't agree with that," and she blinked.

She watched him frown as he listened, and then he asked abruptly, "Why don't I agree? That would take some explaining."

Cathy expected Mrs. Smithson to terminate the conversation, but she didn't.

Finally he said, "Of course I'd be willing to meet with you and talk your idea over, even though I can tell you right now that I don't think I could become involved in a project like that. But . . . I am at a disadvantage. My hands were burned—slightly—and for the time being I'm not able to drive."

Cathy nudged Jed, and he excused himself and clapped a bandaged hand over the mouthpiece.

"If you need transportation," she said sweetly, "Eduardo is available. He drove the judge's car down from Boston, remember, and I'm sure he would be delighted to take you anywhere you want to go."

"That's okay," Jed mumbled, and turned back to the phone.

"Two o'clock tomorrow afternoon will be fine," he said. "I'll look forward to seeing you then."

Cathy took the phone from him, and he sat back.

"I won't need to ask Eduardo to drive me," he informed her. "Mrs. Smithson is sending her car and chauffeur for me."

He grinned. "She's quite something. You have to give her A+ for imagination. She has this nutty idea of using a big tract of land she owns here on the Cape for a rest home/hospital complex for dogs. I guess you heard me tell her there's no way I could go along with anything like that...."

Baffled, Cathy asked, "What would you have to do with it?"

"She'd like me to come up with a plan for what she has in mind, and if we're in tune with each other at that point she'd be interested in having me build it."

"Jed," Cathy said, moving cautiously on this, "you might at least give the idea some serious consideration."

He laughed. "No way, Cathy. Much as I like dogs, I could never get involved in something like that. I'd be haunted by all the kids in the world who need food in their stomachs and clothes on their backs."

"Jed, Genevieve Smithson is a very wealthy woman."

"So?"

"She is a *very* wealthy woman."

He scowled. "What does that have to do with anything?"

"A lot, maybe. I'm not about to violate any lawyer-client confidences, but I *can* tell you that she has been seriously thinking about leaving her entire estate to Sylvester, who happens to be her dog."

"She mentioned that," Jed admitted. "Evidently you told her that even if Sylvester outlived her he might not outlive her by very long."

"Yes, I did."

"You asked her who'd inherit from Sylvester, and she said that's had her thinking."

"Thank God for small favors," Cathy muttered.

"That's why she's come up with the idea of a canine center that can be named after Sylvester. She figures that if she dies before he does, he could live there in maximum comfort for the rest of his life. Then other dogs would inherit the best of everything from him."

"All right, I agree with you that it's a zany idea," Cathy acknowledged. "But it's a step in a better direction than leaving everything outright to Sylvester. Anyway, I personally think Genevieve Smithson is going to outlive all the dogs in the world."

"You don't like her, do you?"

Cathy was surprised. She said slowly, "It's not a question of liking or disliking her, Jed. She's my client. I feel it my responsibility to give her advice that I, at least, consider logical.

"All right, before you say anything—no, I don't think this idea of establishing a canine center and endowing it with millions is logical. I agree with you— there are too many suffering people in the world, especially children. But it may be the best thing I can convince Mrs. Smithson to do. We've been going back and forth about her will for months now.''

''I take it she wants to change whatever will she had before she made her plans for Sylvester?''

Cathy nodded. ''That's right. Her money was to go to a great-nephew who was killed during the Persian Gulf War, and he was the last of her line.''

Cathy sighed. ''I can see where she's coming from. She's old, she's lonely, she inherited wealth and then married wealth. She's never had any children of her own. I imagine many people, over the years, have used her—or tried to—because of her money. She's been hurt, I'm sure, and she doesn't trust people easily. So she has more faith in dogs than she does in humans, which is pretty sad.

''If it would please her, the canine center might be a viable solution for her,'' Cathy decided. ''In that case, there's no reason why you shouldn't work with her, Jed.''

He snarled, ''The hell there isn't. I'm not about to pull out of my financial mess by fleecing a woman like Genevieve Smithson, Cathy. She doesn't deserve that kind of treatment.''

''No,'' Cathy had to agree, ''she doesn't. But if you don't work with her, you can bet someone else will. And probably would really fleece her.''

''Then it'll be on their conscience.''

Eduardo announced lunch. He had fixed a magnificent frittata that Jed could handle with the tongs, and he was delighted when Jed accepted a second helping.

Cathy had come home to check on Jed and have lunch with him. Now there was no reason for her to linger—and, as far as her profession was concerned, every reason why she shouldn't. Her workload hadn't lessened.

She extracted a promise from Jed that he wouldn't go over to Cedarville on his own, and then went back to her office. But never, since she first started practice, had she been less interested in the fascinating challenges of the law.

Don Crandon called her late in the afternoon, and asked if they could go to lunch the next day.

"A few details I'd like to discuss with you," he said.

Cathy thought about missing a lunch with Jed. But he'd be leaving early in the afternoon for his appointment with Mrs. Smithson and, anyway, she did want to talk with Don. Without Jed present, she could be more forthright than she might have been otherwise, and perhaps she'd be able to wheedle some information out of Don, too.

She accepted the lunch invitation.

The judge was her next caller. "Has Eduardo settled in?" he asked her.

"He hasn't merely settled in, I think by now he just about owns the place."

The judge chuckled. "Don't tell him, but I feel like a kid who's having a great time playing hooky. This morning I had chocolate ice cream with peanuts sprinkled over it for breakfast."

"Dad!"

A thought struck Cathy. Many of the people who got in trouble in Middlesex County came before her father in court, and those he didn't deal with personally he heard about.

"Does the name DiAngelo mean anything to you?" she asked him.

"It's not an uncommon name," the judge pointed out. "Do you have a first name?"

"Well, the father of the men I'm thinking about was named Tony. He owned a successful contracting business in Somerville, and had a hand in a few other enterprises, as well. He died a couple of years ago. I understand his three sons took over the business—two of them, anyway. One is named Benny, then there's Sam, and the one I'm not so sure about is Mario."

"Is Jed involved with these people?" the judge asked.

"He was. No longer. But there's been bad feeling, and there's a chance one of them still may have it in for Jed."

"I'll put Marcia Jackson on this," the judge promised. "She's clerking for me, and she's good. It may take a little digging. Suppose I bring whatever she comes up with along when I come down Thursday."

"That would be terrific, Dad."

"How *is* Jed?"

"Getting restless. Sometimes I think we have a caged tiger on our hands. Eduardo's great with him. Jed is more receptive to asking Eduardo for help than he is to asking Gladys or me."

"Moriarty's young, strong—he'll be fine," the judge said.

As Cathy finished her conversation with her father and got back to work, she remembered that Gladys had voiced that same opinion.

She was about to call it a day when the phone rang again, and this time it was Bill, who wanted to be updated on Jed.

After Cathy had given him the latest progress report, she said, "I'm about to take off. Why don't I get

Jed, and we'll both come over and see you. Not for long, though. When Eduardo sets a dinner time, it's carved in stone.''

"I've got some news of my own," Bill said. "So come along."

When Cathy got home, Jed was sitting at the kitchen table, sipping a fruit-juice concoction prepared by Eduardo.

The two men were talking, and Cathy realized after a second that they were speaking Spanish.

Surprised, she said, "I didn't know you spoke Spanish, Jed."

"I don't," Jed said. "I know a few words, that's all. There are a lot of Hispanic people working in construction up around Somerville."

"El señor habla muy bien," Eduardo insisted.

"Yes," Cathy said. "I imagine the *señor* does speak very well, Eduardo. But the *señor* is also extremely modest. He is not inclined to toot his own horn."

"¿Perdón?" Eduardo asked blankly.

Cathy made a laughing explanation while Jed frowned at her. Then she asked Eduardo if she and Jed had time to make a brief hospital visit to a friend.

"One hour and a half," Eduardo said firmly, and Cathy made a show out of looking at her watch and synchronizing it with the clock on the kitchen wall.

Once she and Jed were in her car and on their way, she said, "It's true, you know. You do play yourself down."

"No reason to play myself up." Quickly Jed added, "How did your afternoon go?"

"I'm glad it's over," she admitted.

She wanted to tell him she'd thought about him constantly, couldn't wait to get back to him. But there was a reserve about Jed at the moment that made her decide maybe this wasn't the best moment to get too personal.

"Incidentally," she said, "I'm meeting Don Crandon for lunch tomorrow."

"Am I supposed to go with you?"

"Well ... no."

"I gather it doesn't work both ways."

"What?"

"You insist that you sit in on any discussion I have with any of those people. The reverse doesn't hold."

"Jed, Don wants to get some information from me, and I hope I can persuade him to share with me some of what he's put together. Frankly, it would be better if you weren't there."

"A strictly professional conference, eh?"

Cathy asked impatiently, "What is it with you?"

He didn't answer her.

She turned into the hospital parking lot, thankful that they could get out of this conversation ... for a little while, anyway.

The lot was crowded. Cathy had to park at the back, and she and Jed started toward the main building, maintaining a stiff silence.

Then he stopped and glanced skyward. Following his gaze, Cathy saw that the sky was indigo and the stars were like brilliant jewels embedded in a perfect setting.

"The air's so much clearer down here than it is around Somerville," Jed murmured. "Look at the Dipper...."

Cathy did look at the stars, but then her focus shifted to Jed. He was standing with his shoulders thrown back, his legs slightly apart. She traced his big, powerful body with her eyes, and felt that aching mix of desire and . . . yes, love.

They were the last two people in the world who belonged together, no doubt about it, she thought, misery mixing with aching need. But what a gap there was going to be in her life when he was gone.

He was a constant challenge. She was never sure what was going to happen next between them. The two of them struck sparks off each other even when they were at the edge of making love.

She saw that he'd turned from stargazing and was looking at her.

"I'm sorry I made such a federal case out of your having lunch with Crandon," he said. "The fact is that the thought of it makes me jealous as hell."

Cathy knew he would have reached for her then, if he could have. As it was, he bent and brushed her lips with a sweetness that made her yearn for more. Then, nudging her with his arm, he said, "Come on, or we'll never manage to see Bill and make it back to the house in time to suit Eduardo."

Cathy's senses were still spinning as they took the elevator up to Bill's floor. Bill was sitting out in the corridor in his wheelchair, and he beamed when he saw them.

"I'm out of here tomorrow," he told them enthusiastically. On a slightly more subdued note, he added, "That doesn't mean I'm about to start dancing in the near future. It'll be a while before I can get back to the office, Cathy, but no reason why you can't pass along some of the workload pretty soon. I was thinking I could even see some clients at home. We have an enclosed all-weather porch that could be converted into a temporary office.''

Bill grinned. ''Clients like Jed, for instance,'' he said.

Cathy spoke before she realized he was teasing her. ''I'm pretty deep into Jed's case at this point, Bill,'' she said, and flushed when Bill laughed.

Jed and Cathy got back to her house with only minutes to spare, if they were to keep to Eduardo's timetable. He had lighted the candles in the dining room, fixed a fresh floral centerpiece, and he presented them with a gourmet dinner that would have done credit to a master chef. Again, he had taken care not to make anything that would require much dexterity on Jed's part.

The meal was so delicious that Cathy wished she had invited Gladys to share it with them. Having Gladys around would have been a kind of safeguard between Jed and herself, too, she thought, as she and Jed drifted into the living room where Eduardo served them cappuccino.

She had to smile at the idea that she and Jed needed a chaperon.

You're a big girl, Catherine, she reminded herself, *and you're going to have to learn to deal with Moriarty all by yourself.*

The object of her speculations was sitting at the opposite end of the couch, carefully juggling a fragile coffee cup and doing a good job of it.

Looking at Jed's bandaged hands, Cathy asked, ''Do you want a pain pill?''

"No," Jed said. "Why? Do I look like I'm hurting?"

"There's no point to suffering needlessly, Jed."

Jed smiled wryly. "Pain pills wouldn't do much for the kind of hurt I'm feeling." Shrugging, he admitted, "Yeah, there comes a point when I start hurting when I'm with you, Cathy, because I want you so damned much, and I know that's not the way either of us should be going. Things got out of hand between us the other night...."

Cathy couldn't believe what she was hearing. Jed didn't *regret* what had happened, did he?

His smile was sad. "Don't look like that," he said, and added perceptively, "If I live to be a thousand, the memory of you in my arms will remain a miracle to me. But that doesn't mean we should become lovers."

Cathy said tightly, "I thought we did become lovers, Jed."

He shook his head slowly. "No," he said. "The other night was a miracle, like I said, and...you can't expect miracles to repeat themselves."

"Are you saying that you and I only had the capacity to make love once, Jed?"

"No," he ground out.

He tried not to look at Cathy as he made that admission, but he couldn't help himself. She had taken off her suit jacket, but she was still wearing the skirt and blouse she'd worn to work. It was a beautiful blouse, soft satin with long sleeves and a flowing bow that tied at the neck. Gold earrings glittered on Cathy's ears. She'd nibbled off most of her lipstick, her nose was shiny, her hair tumbled wildly around her shoulders. Jed's pulse thumped. Cathy had to be the most enticing, most sexy woman in the whole world.

"Think you can make love with two bandaged hands?" she asked him.

He stared at her.

"Let's prove that miracles can happen twice, Jed," she said, her tone almost flippant. But then her voice lowered, and she didn't sound nearly so sure of herself as she murmured, "I've never in my life said this to a man before, but I want you so much...."

She was like a candle lighting his way. Jed followed her up the stairs and into her bedroom.

She switched on a lamp, and a rosy glow spread across the bedspread and the pillowcases. Cathy slipped off her skirt and shrugged off her blouse and then slowly pulled off her panty hose. And as Jed saw one beautiful tapered leg emerge and then the other, his throat felt parched.

Cathy teased, "You need some help." And as she began to undress him, Jed discovered that there could be advantages to having two bandaged hands.

Cathy took off his clothes with exquisite care. As she worked on buttons and buckles, her hands roved and explored with a tantalizing slowness that was the essence of provocation.

Her fingers fondled his bare chest, further mussing the mat of black curls. She trailed her hands over his hips as she tugged off his jeans, then she slid her fingers beneath the elastic on his briefs. And as her hands followed their downward course, Jed's self-control began to shatter.

Cathy's heart was beating like a sledgehammer. Even the other night, she hadn't done *this*. And though she'd seen his male magnificence then, she was newly staggered by it and startled by the power of her fingers.

They sank down on the bed together. Jed's eyes were glazed and he was breathing fast as she caressed him, and she wanted it to be like that. As much as she desired him, she wanted this to be *his* night. She knew that he couldn't touch her intimately, as he had before. She didn't expect to be aroused now in the way she had been then. But she was wrong.

Jed moved over Cathy, and made love to her with his mouth, his body and his strong, wonderful arms, and they began their climb to the stars together. And once they'd tumbled over the edge of the universe and their breathing gradually came back to normal, they realized that, tonight, they'd gone way, way beyond the Dipper.

Chapter Twelve

"I called a ten-minute recess so I could phone you," the judge told Cathy.

"Does that mean you've found out something about the DiAngelos?"

"No, though it wouldn't surprise me to see the youngest one come before me one of these days."

"Dad, what *have* you found out?"

The judge's dramatic style was going to drive her crazy some day, Cathy decided.

"Sam, the oldest brother, has headed the construction company since Tony DiAngelo died," the judge said. "Benny is his right-hand man. They seem to have divested themselves of their father's other business interests.

"Mario is the youngest...."

"I know that."

"The two older brothers have tried to involve him in the company, but he has problems."

"What kinds of problems?"

"He's an alcoholic, for one," the judge said. "Evidently he's into drugs, at least to some extent, though he's never been caught with anything. He's had a couple of short stays in a private mental hospital, which appear to have been primarily to dry him out. But Marcia says there are indications of some emotional instability."

"Enough emotional instability so he'd start a vendetta against Jed?"

"It's possible, Cathy. Marcia will keep working on this. I get the picture that Sam and Benny DiAngelo are solid citizens, respected on the local business scene and well entrenched in community life. Mario appears to be a different story, and I want a profile on him."

It was Wednesday morning, and Cathy was at her desk. She fingered her gold pen and asked anxiously, "Do you know where Mario DiAngelo is, Dad? Where he lives, or where he might be right now?"

"He lives with Sam and his wife most of the time. But that doesn't mean much, Cathy. The Cape is such an easy run from Somerville."

The judge paused, then said, "The bailiff's at the door. I'd better get back to the courtroom. I hope to have more for you tomorrow."

"Thanks a lot, Dad." Her voice softened. "I love you, Judge."

She hung up the phone and tapped the pen against the desk blotter.

Mario DiAngelo *could* be responsible for a vicious hate campaign against Jed. She didn't want to leap to conclusions, but Mario did have a motive.

Cathy put the pen aside, and asked Gladys to send in the next client.

The rest of the morning was busy, and it was almost one when Cathy left the office to drive across the Cape to the bayside restaurant where she was to meet Don Crandon.

They sat on an enclosed deck with a view of a busy harbor, and watched the fishing boats heading out on the tide. The Cape was new to him, Crandon confessed, and everything about it fascinated him. He was from Chicago, and had been in Boston less than a year.

"With no vacation time so far," he said. "And it'll be a long time before I can take a real holiday if the number of suspected arson cases keeps mounting. I'd like to come down here and go whale-watching, for one thing."

"Whale-watching is a great experience," Cathy said. "The weather's getting a bit on the cold side for it now, though."

"Well, I'm in the market for sight-seeing, too. You wouldn't want to volunteer as a guide, would you?"

He kept the question light enough so it didn't sound too much like trying to make a date.

"Right now I don't even have time to look at the view from my own house," Cathy told him, and then elaborated about Bill's accident and her office situation.

They were sipping coffee by the time they got around to talking about Jed Moriarty. They were now on a first-name basis, and Cathy was sure that her first impressions of Don Crandon had been right. He was a shrewd investigator, thorough; he would leave nothing to chance.

She was tempted to tell him about her conversation with the judge earlier, and even to suggest that perhaps he might want to look into Mario DiAngelo's background himself. But she decided to table that until she'd talked to her father again.

Instead, she said earnestly, "Don, there's no way Jed Moriarty would have set those fires himself."

"I want to believe that," Crandon confessed, "but I have to keep an open mind on the subject."

"I appreciate that. Even so..."

"Moriarty fits the pattern of a present-day arsonist so perfectly." Crandon looked grim. "That's the problem. With the heavy financial burden he's shouldering, it's easy to assume that he tried to take what's becoming a standard way out."

"No," Cathy insisted. "Jed waited too long to get that land, and he worked too hard on those first two spec houses."

She drew a long breath. "Even if that weren't true, you have to admit he would have been an idiot to blow up his trailer while he was inside it."

"Stranger things have happened," Crandon said wryly. "Moriarty could have paid someone to toss that contraption into his trailer. He could have figured that forewarned was forearmed. I'm saying he could have believed that since he knew what was coming he could escape with minor injuries at the worst. But the plan backfired."

"Don," Cathy prodded, "do you believe that? If you do, I'm afraid we don't have much to talk about.

I have absolute confidence in Jed Moriarty's integrity."

"He's a lucky man to have an attorney like you." Crandon looked at her in admiration as he spoke. "But I tend to play devil's advocate when I'm looking for information," he admitted. "In my business, facts have to come before gut feelings. But the moment does sometimes arrive when you have to go with your gut feeling, and I think you're right about Jed Moriarty. I, too, don't believe he would have sabotaged himself. So I'm going to get him off the hook."

Cathy gave Crandon a broad smile.

"That's terrific," she said. "Especially if your report will prod the insurance company into paying up."

"It will push them," Crandon conceded. "Moriarty should get paybacks on the two houses that were torched last summer, the trailer and the various items around his place that were vandalized. I've studied his financial picture, and I doubt what he'll get back will put him in the black, which is unfortunate. But he should be okay if he can start working again before too long."

"That's the big question," Cathy admitted soberly.

"I know. I talked to his doctor. It maybe be quite a while before he's able to use his hands for anything like building, and even then..."

Cathy didn't want to think about the "even then." A mix of helplessness and hopelessness threatened to swamp her. It would be such an intolerable handicap.

"Cathy," Crandon said consolingly, seeming to see into her heart, "I'll do everything I can to persuade the insurance company to expedite things for Moriarty."

"That would be great of you, Don."

Cathy thought again of telling Don Crandon about Mario DiAngelo. But she wanted to have something a bit more concrete to go on, if possible. If the judge didn't find out anything more about the youngest DiAngelo, then she would get in touch with Crandon and tell him what she knew.

It was two-thirty when Cathy got back to her office. She knew that Jed would be at Genevieve Smithson's by now, and she tried to picture the two of them together. She was sure that Mrs. Smithson had never in her eighty years of living met anyone quite like Jed Moriarty.

Few people had.

As she drove home that evening, she realized she was so eager to see Jed, that nothing else mattered—and she knew she was going to have to put a rein on her feelings. Jed was not going to be her star boarder forever. One of these days he would be gone, and she'd be walking into an empty house again.

At the thought of that, Cathy felt the well of loneliness deep inside her that she seldom acknowledged, and the waters threatened to become very deep.

When she walked into her living room and found Jed watching TV, she was so glad to see him that she stood on the threshold for a minute and just watched him.

He was wearing his red sweater and the new snug-fitting jeans. Looking at him was enough to bring desire out of hiding, and the brew that began to flow through Cathy was sharp and hot.

Jed turned and saw her, and he got up and came across the room to her. Cathy went into his arms as naturally as if she'd found the place where she'd always belonged. He held her close and she pillowed her head against his chest, letting the nearness and the goodness of him weave a spell over her.

Jed said huskily, "I missed you today."

Cathy looked up at him and let herself drown a little in his deep blue eyes; she wished it could be like this every night for the rest of her life. She wanted Jed to be here to greet her, she wanted him to be part of her existence through eternity....

The magnitude of what she was thinking suddenly struck her, and instinctively she eased herself out of Jed's arms, saw his puzzled expression and veered to a safer subject.

"How was the meeting with Genevieve Smithson?" she asked.

Jed smiled. "She's quite a lady."

They sat down on the couch together; close, but not too close.

"Mrs. Smithson said she's going to mull over what we talked about and get back to me."

Cathy was intrigued. "And what might that have been?"

"Well, I told her I could understand how she feels about Sylvester—who happens to be a terrific dog, incidentally. He's a Sheltie—in Scotland they use his breed to herd sheep.

"Anyway...I told her how much I've always wanted to have a dog, and that someday I plan to have at least one."

Jed hesitated. "She asked me if I had ever had a dog when I was growing up...."

His voice trailed off, and his eyes seemed clouded by memories.

Cathy prodded gently, "Then?"

"I explained to her that in the part of Somerville where I lived, there was no way I could have had a dog. The traffic was so bad he would have been killed in five minutes. Then we moved in with my uncle, and I had no chance at all. He hated animals.

"It's a strange coincidence," Jed allowed, "but Mrs. Smithson told me her father hated animals. When she was a little girl, a friend of the family gave her a puppy for Christmas. Her father got rid of it. She never forgave him—which I can damn well understand. But..."

"Yes?"

"I told her that while I understand how she feels about Sylvester, there are more important considerations in the world than dogs."

Cathy's eyes widened. "Wow!"

Jed grinned. "We got onto the subject of other animals, and she shuddered when I mentioned cats. She is not a cat lover. Horses, yes. She did a lot of riding when she was younger. And she could see having ponies around for kids.

"That's what I was getting at," Jed admitted. "I told her that as far as I'm concerned, children are more important than dogs, cats, horses, or even adults."

"And she didn't toss you right out of the house?"

"You underestimate her, Cathy."

"I don't know. Evidently, she never wanted to have children herself."

"You're wrong. She wanted to have children more than she wanted anything else in life. But when she was twenty she was in an accident, and they had to do a hysterectomy. She said probably it would have been avoided today, but we're talking sixty years ago."

Cathy stared at him. "She told you that?"

"Yes. She said she knew that later she could have adopted children. She and her husband sometimes talked about it, but they never did it."

Jed watched Cathy's face as he spoke, and he saw a clear message written on it.

Bill and Gladys had both told him how much Cathy wanted children, and right now that was plain to see. So plain that Jed was disturbed.

She wanted children so much she could easily make a terrible mistake. She had a few years left for child-bearing, but not that many. Time passed quickly, and Jed feared that the closer it came to running out, the more Cathy would be apt to push a panic button.

It would be a hell of a mess for her if she went into a wrong marriage in order to satisfy her maternal instinct.

Jed thought about Cathy marrying someone primarily so she could have kids, and he couldn't stand the idea of that happening. Cathy deserved so much more. She deserved a man who would love her and cherish her for herself alone. Someone she would love and cherish in return. Someone who would be everything to her as she would be to him—for *their* sakes, not only because of the children they might have.

Jed saw Cathy flex her shoulders, and he knew she was tense as well as tired.

"Go on," she urged. "What else did you and Mrs. Smithson get into?"

"She wants me to see the land she's talking about. It's a big tract overlooking Nantucket Sound. From the way she describes it, I'd think it would make a wonderful center for children. It could be a place for children from the inner city to come and spend not just a couple of weeks, but a whole summer.

"I pointed out that an experience like that could change the course of so many lives. The kids would see a whole new world. They'd learn that there really are things in life apart from crime and filth and hunger and other kinds of misery."

Moved, Cathy asked, "What did she say?"

"Well, she said that no one had ever suggested anything like that before, and she wanted to know if there'd be a place for animals in the center. I told her of course there would be. The center could be a year-round haven for animals. But I thought there should be different kinds of animals there, not just dogs.

"When the kids were around, the kids would have the animals and the animals would have the kids. Matter of fact, it might be possible to have a winter program as well as a summer one for inner-city children. Or maybe the center could be run year-round in three- or four-month segments. Arrangements would have to be made for schooling for the kids in off-vacation time, but that would be possible. I can imagine a lot of teachers would grab the chance to work in a setup like the one I'm thinking about."

"You are...dazzling me," Cathy admitted.

Jed chuckled. "Mrs. Smithson seemed to be daz-zled, too. She said the concept is mind-boggling, and it's all she's going to be able to think about. After she's done some thinking, she'll get back to me. There was a real spark in her eyes, Cathy."

Jed finished quietly, "She's quite a person. It's too bad most people don't seem able to see the woman behind the money."

Cathy's emotions were in such high gear that it was almost a relief to have Eduardo bring wine and a tray of hors d'oeuvres.

As Jed munched a canapé, he said wryly, "This kind of life is going to spoil me."

Cathy's voice was soft. "I don't think anything could ever spoil you, Jed Moriarty."

That was so true.

She felt a surge of admiration for Genevieve Smithson. Mrs. Smithson had appreciated Jed's good looks, bless her, but she'd also seen the man behind the handsome facade.

Chagrined, Cathy knew she couldn't say the same of herself, in the beginning.

She thought of her first reaction to Jed, and she felt that she'd been a narrow-minded little snob.

Jed Moriarty was real treasure.

What an idiot Angela DiAngelo must have been!

Jed asked gently, "What's the problem?"

"Problem?" Cathy echoed.

"You look angry and unhappy all at once."

Cathy hedged, "I guess I'm tired, that's all."

"Mmm . . . speaking of today's appointments, how did your lunch with Crandon go?"

"Don's going to turn in a positive report on you, and he thinks the insurance company will pay off."

"Your powers of persuasion must have been pretty great."

"The facts spoke for themselves, Jed."

She went on, "If you get the insurance money, it will be a big help to you. But you'll need more than that to stay out of the hole. I hope Mrs. Smithson will give you a green light on this project. If that happens, it would be a good idea to put Cranberry Estates aside for the time being. A contract for the Smithson project would really pull you through."

Jed said, "I was not offering Mrs. Smithson a business proposition, Cathy. There is such a thing as wanting to do something for somebody without making money on it."

Cathy drew back. "I don't like the way you put that." Smarting, she challenged, "Do you think I'm out to make money from your case, Moriarty? Do you think that's why I want you to work out something profitable with Genevieve Smithson?"

"Of course not." Jed looked disgusted.

Cathy persisted. "You will *never* receive another bill from Abernathy, Crowell and DiNatale. I guarantee that."

"Even if we don't get things settled between us for years and years and years?" he asked.

She had to look at him. He was smiling, and that steady blue gaze swamped her.

Before she could decide what to say to him, he switched subjects again.

"Cathy," he said, "I really need to go over to Cedarville tomorrow. I have to see what's left . . . for myself. I thought that if you didn't object I'd ask Eduardo to drive me."

"No," she said, and added wearily, "I've already told you, I don't want you going to Cedarville without me, Jed."

"Give me a couple reasons why not, will you? You said Crandon is going to write a favorable report to the insurance agency."

"Even so, I don't feel that you're home free yet. I trust Don. But the insurance company has to agree with him before anything's done, and there is still a possible margin for error."

She brushed a strand of bronze hair back from her forehead. "If you feel so strongly about it, I'll arrange to drive over to Cedarville with you tomorrow afternoon."

"I'm not asking that of you," Jed protested.

"I know. I'm volunteering."

Cathy looked so damned tired, Jed decided against getting into even a small argument with her, and let his instincts take over. He moved closer to her, put his arm around her and pulled her toward him.

He nibbled her earlobes, traced the pearly rim of her ear with the tip of his tongue and felt her shiver.

He murmured, "After dinner, let's go to bed. Same bed. All right? For tonight, let's forget about everything except each other."

Cathy was learning that when she was with Jed there was a fire deep inside her that was never entirely banked. Now the embers ignited, and the effect was like a sizzling flame that kept getting wider and wider and hotter and hotter.

Jed, his voice low, urged, "This time—do something, will you? I'd have to ask Eduardo to drive me to the pharmacy, and that would be pretty obvious. But you..."

He could feel her stiffen in his arms, and wished he'd kept his mouth shut. But though he wanted Cathy desperately, the voice of caution nagged at him.

Twice, now, they'd taken a risk. No matter how much she might want a child, he didn't want anything to happen... that way.

Were she to become pregnant, he'd marry her, of course. But that wasn't what he wanted. He'd be the proudest, the happiest man in the world if he could be the father of Cathy Merrill's child. But not under the kind of circumstances that would follow if they trusted to blind luck much more often.

She had to want him first as a man, not because he could give her a baby. She had to love him for himself. Otherwise, whatever there was between them could never last.

Cathy pulled away, and Jed wanted her back so badly that he could have given in, if she'd let him. But she might as well have turned a cold shower on both of them as she said, "It won't be necessary for either of us to go anywhere.

"I brought home some work I need to finish, and I'm sure you can find something to occupy you." There was ice in Cathy's voice. "As for Cedarville— I'll see to it that my schedule is cleared tomorrow afternoon so that we can go over there together, and get it over with."

Chapter Thirteen

The reality of seeing Jed's charred trailer was even worse than Cathy had expected it would be.

She trembled as she stared at the twisted black skeleton. She could think only of what *might* have happened.

She could have lost Jed. He could have been killed in the terrible inferno that had consumed the trailer. Now, as she looked at the wreckage, she thought that his having gotten out in time had to have been a miracle.

The door, she learned, had been jammed. Jed had managed to get it open only with sheer, brute strength. His hands were already burned. He'd had to depend on his arms and shoulders and he'd wrenched his left shoulder—something he had kept from her. But that was enough to make her wonder how much he was keeping to himself.

She, Jed, Don Crandon, the Cedarville police chief and a member of the arson squad, were standing in the clearing next to the horribly warped ruins.

Cathy commented in a low tone meant for Jed's ears only, "It's a wonder you didn't *break* your shoulder when you crashed the door."

She had to strain to hear his answer. "I guess the adrenaline flow was pretty strong."

She slanted a glance at him. He sounded more on edge that he looked. He *looked* impassive as a rock, and just as strong. But she knew he had to be churning inside.

She thought about the possessions he'd lost in the explosion—the duck decoy and the turquoise insulator and the leather-bound books. They weren't all that valuable, but they were all he had. And his plans for Cranberry Estates had gone up in flames, too.

She knew he didn't have much money in the bank. And the clothes he and Gladys had bought—plus what he'd been wearing when he was taken to the emergency room—were all he had. Her house was his for as long as he might want to use it, but essentially he was homeless. The insurance money, when it came through, would help him get a start again, but it wouldn't be enough. And both of his hands—the real tools of his trade—were injured and right now of no use to him.

Cathy marveled that he could hold his head high, in view of the circumstances. She wouldn't have blamed him for caving in and yielding to the depression that certainly must trail him constantly and be ever ready to overwhelm him.

She glanced at him again. He was holding his head *very* high.

God, but I admire your guts, Moriarty.

Cathy wished she could speak the words aloud. Sometime she would.

She heard the police chief say, "Is there anything you could add to your description of that pickup?"

Jed shook his head. "Not really. I've seldom gotten much more than a glimpse of it, and the license plate was so grimy that there was no way I could read it."

His brow furrowed. "There's a bad ding in the rear bumper—I'm not sure I told you that. It's a fairly old model—-either a Chevy or a Ford, I'm not certain."

"Do you think it has a Massachusetts license plate?"

"I suspect so. The background is light—or would be, if the plate were washed. The letters are spaced like Massachusetts license-plate numbers."

The chief frowned. "It's a wonder he hasn't been picked up just on the plate alone."

"I suspect he uses back roads and maybe only travels at night."

"That's what we think, and we're putting out special night patrols. Mr. Moriarty, if you remember anything else, no matter how trivial it may seem, get in touch."

"Yeah," Jed said, "I'll get in touch."

Cathy heard the edge of cynicism, and couldn't blame Jed. He'd had to damn near get himself killed to have any of these people believe him.

She addressed Crandon. "Don, if we're not needed for anything else, I think Mr. Moriarty and I will take off."

"I'd say that's all for now, Cathy."

"Will you be staying on the Cape much longer?"

He looked surprised. "Probably not. I'll write my report back in Boston. Why?"

Cathy saw that Jed was looking at her as if he, too, wondered why it should matter to her whether or not Don Crandon was staying on the Cape.

She said, thinking of the judge, "I may have some information I might want to share with you."

Crandon reached for his wallet, and handed her a business card. "I'll be at the Holiday Inn in Hyannis through tonight," he said, "and I should be in my Boston office by late tomorrow morning. Leave a message if I'm not there, and I'll get right back to you."

"Good."

Cathy was about to say goodbye to the others when Jed interrupted.

"I want to look at the house before I leave," he said. "I'd like to make sure myself that everything's okay."

Cathy couldn't blame him, but she personally couldn't wait to get away from Cranberry Estates, especially from the scorched trailer. But she trudged alongside Jed as he surveyed every inch of the house he was building, and only then was he satisfied that no damage had been done to it.

Late-afternoon shadows were draping the Cape by the time Cathy and Jed drove away from the development. And the play of shades between light and darkness echoed Cathy's mood.

Jed was silent, and she could read nothing from his face. She imagined that he was once again deciding that he had to go it alone, and was determined to do his damnedest to work out his problems by himself.

She wondered if he would ever learn about sharing? Could she ever bring him around to believing that when someone cared about a person they wanted to share that person's bad times as well as their good times, wanted to be involved in problems as well as pleasures?

Jed said abruptly, "Drive over to Route 28, will you please, Cathy?"

"Something special you want?" she asked. She had planned to head in the opposite direction, and take the Mid Cape highway back to Hyannis.

"There are some motels along 28," he said. "I don't think there'll be any trouble getting a room this time of year, but I'd like to check out prices."

"Are you speaking about booking a motel unit for yourself?" Cathy tried to keep her annoyance with him from boiling into anger.

He nodded.

She wanted to shake him, but she forced herself to speak calmly. "May I ask why?"

"That should be obvious. I can't go sponging on you."

"Oh, please," she protested. "To begin with, you're not sponging on me. Anyway, we both have enough to think about right now without getting into *that*."

"Cathy, I'm serious."

Cathy pulled over to the side of the road, turned off the motor and faced him.

"Okay," she allowed, "if you're serious, I will be, too. Stop and consider how foolish it would be for you to strike out by yourself right now, Jed. You still need help."

His jawline tightened. "Thanks for reminding me."

"You act as though I'm trying to rub it in. You should know that's not so. Just use a little common sense. Help is available, so avail yourself of it."

"I have."

Jed's face was turned away from her; he was staring through the window at a straggly pine tree struggling for life on the side of the road.

"I don't want you to misunderstand this," he said. "I will never forget what you've done for me. I don't know what I can ever do for *you* to ever begin to compensate. But now it's time for me to move on."

"Move on?" she echoed.

"Yes. I have a lot of things to straighten out, Cathy."

"Tell me about them." It was hard not to glare at him. "I thought that my job involved helping you straighten out the things you're talking about."

"You've done more than enough for me already."

"That's a matter of opinion."

"It's the way I feel," Jed admitted. "I asked Eduardo if he'd be free tonight to drive me back over here."

"And what did Eduardo say?"

"He said okay."

"Does he have any idea what you're actually asking of him?"

"I didn't spell it out, no."

Cathy's temper was wearing thin. "You know damned well that if Eduardo agrees to help you get stashed in some motel room, I . . . I'm going to ask my father to fire him," she sputtered.

"Come on," Jed protested. "That would really be unfair."

"Who are you to say anything about being fair?" The more impassive Jed became, the more Cathy felt she was going to lose control. "Have you been uncomfortable in my house?"

"Uncomfortable?" Jed looked as if she'd just spoken to him in a foreign language. "How could I have been uncomfortable? You, Gladys, Eduardo... you've all been terrific to me."

He tried to smile. "That's part of the problem, don't you see?"

"No, I don't see."

"Cathy... right now I'm just about flat broke. I have a long way to go before I can hope to put my act together again. Until that happens, there's no way I can pay you back. Try to understand that, will you?"

Cathy glared at him. "Are you talking about money?"

He shook his head. "No. Of course I'm not talking about money. I could never pay you back with *money*. Don't you think I know that? But I can't accept any more from you until I can do something for you. And right now, there's not a damned thing I can do for you. I hope, someday, that'll change. But until it does, if it ever does, I have to get along by myself."

Cathy closed her eyes, not daring to look at him.

Didn't he have any idea of how much she loved him?

She wanted him not for just a night but forever. Cathy's eyes stung with hot tears as she thought about that. She wanted a little girl who would have Jed's curly black hair and those same astonishing blue eyes. She wanted a little boy who would look like Jed but would have her coloring. She didn't give a damn if it took Jed *years* of building beautiful houses for people to become as successful as she was sure he'd be. She'd had all the material things anyone could want ever since she could remember. She didn't need *things* from Jed. She needed him.

Her voice was slightly husky as she said, "I understand how you feel."

Jed blinked. "What was that?"

"I understand how you feel, Jed."

He was instantly suspicious. "You're saying you'll go along with what I want to do?"

"Yes. If that really is what you want to do."

She turned the key in the ignition switch.

"I'll drive over to Route 28 and you can check out some motels if you like," she agreed. "But let's stop somewhere and get a cup of coffee first, okay? I don't know about you, but I'm cold."

Jed slumped back in the seat. "Okay, sure."

They stopped at a small restaurant, and Cathy indulged in a couple of long swigs of strong black coffee as she tried to decide just how she was going to make Jed see her point of view.

She stirred the coffee, which didn't need stirring, and said casually, "What are you going to do for transportation, Jed?"

"I have the pickup. Fortunately it wasn't parked near enough to the trailer to be damaged much. You may have noticed. The paint's sort of blistered in places, but it should run fine."

She'd noticed the red pickup, but hadn't given it a second thought. She'd been too fixated on the charred trailer.

Now she said, "I shouldn't think you'd be able to drive for a while. That's something you should check out with your doctor. When do you see him again?"

"I saw him this morning."

That was the first she'd heard about him having a doctor's appointment today, and she felt a stab of resentment. He should have told her. Or Eduardo should have.

He read her mind. "Don't start blaming Eduardo again. I asked him not to mention it."

"Why?"

"I didn't want to get into it. Cathy, finish your coffee, will you, so I can stop by a couple of motels before we have to get back for dinner."

"Jed, what did the doctor say about your hands?"

"My right hand is coming along very well. My left hand's not so great. The burns were more severe."

"What do you mean—'not so great'?"

"There may have to be some skin grafting later on. And therapy. It will be important to get the muscles and the tendons working again, and to keep stretching them so they won't tighten up."

As he spoke, Jed hoped Cathy didn't share his vision of a scarred claw for a hand.

He said carefully, "It won't be too long before I can start using my right hand again. I'll certainly be able to drive then. Eventually I should be able to use my left hand. Limited use, maybe, but the doctor keeps telling me that modern medical methods are pretty miraculous, and I believe him. Anyway, I'll make out."

Because it was something that would have to be said sooner or later, and he decided it was better to get it over with now, he added, "Both hands will be scarred.

The left one worse than the right, obviously. But later on I should be able to have plastic surgery that will help with the scars.

"That's more than I could afford right now, of course. But, as I understand it, there's a certain time element involved anyway. The healing process has to be pretty well completed, and—"

Cathy pushed aside her coffee cup, reached across the table and clasped his wrist.

"Moriarty," she said tersely, "I do understand how you feel about staying on at my house. But it's about time you showed some understanding, too. So you might as well know that there's no way in God's world I could live with myself if I actually helped you go motel-hopping until you find a place to stay."

Jed's eyes darkened until they looked as black as midnight. "What made you change your mind? Hearing that I may wind up with a crippled hand? That's pity, Cathy, and who wants it? I don't. Anyway... you don't have to help me go motel-hopping. If that would weigh too heavily on your conscience, I'll call a cab and go by myself."

"Just like you can do everything by yourself, right?" Cathy was hurt, frustrated, seething... all at the same time. "Oh, I don't deny your capabilities, Jed. But right now I'm going to think about myself a little. There's no way I can dump you in some motel and let you try to fend for yourself at this particular point in time."

Her throat felt so tight she could hardly speak. "Dammit, I *care* about you," she grated.

She'd told him that before, Jed remembered, as he lay on the examining table in the emergency room.

He'd reacted then with a rush of emotion he didn't want repeated now. He couldn't afford to lower his guard like that.

Cathy said, "If you care at all about me..."

Care about her? God, Jed thought, he loved her so much it was all he could do to breathe. But there was no way, no way, that he was going to tell her that.

"Jed!"

Jed had been trying not to look at Cathy, but now he had to.

"*Do* you care about me?"

"Of course I care about you," he said unsteadily.

"Okay." Cathy pulled her courage together and went a step further.

"I love you," she said.

Jed reared back as if she had hit him, and shook his head violently. "You can't!"

Cathy felt as if she'd stepped off a cliff and fallen into a bottomless chasm. She hurt all over.

"You are... mixing things up," Jed said.

Her throat ached, her teeth ached, her heart ached. "What are you talking about?" she asked him.

"Cathy... I know what it is that you want."

She stared at him. "What do you think I want?"

"I know how much you want to have kids."

Cathy felt as if her blood were turning to ice water.

"There's nothing wrong with that," Jed added hastily. "But when you speak about love, you're mistaking it for something else."

"A frustrated maternal instinct? Is that what you're saying?"

The hurt was terrible... and getting worse. She felt as if her chest would explode and her lungs would burst at any second.

"Please." Jed had never felt more miserable. "It's not easy to talk to you about this but...it's something that has to be said, Cathy."

Cathy's mind was racing. "You think I made love with you and was careless enough not to—to protect myself because I wanted a child so badly?"

He didn't answer.

Her rage was white hot. "Damn you, Jed Moriarty."

He said unhappily, "I'm more than willing to damn myself. Tell me I'm a bungling idiot. You won't find anyone who could agree with you more. But I have to make you understand...."

Cathy tilted her chin defiantly. "You don't have to make me understand anything, and please don't start apologizing. You said what you think, and I admire honesty."

She glanced at her watch. "We'd better get back to Hyannis. As it is, we're going to be late. I hope you'll string along and let Eduardo serve you dinner tonight. Tomorrow we'll make other arrangements...."

Cathy's eyes suddenly widened and she moaned, "Ohmigod!"

"What is it?" Jed demanded.

"I forgot that the judge is speaking at the Bar Association dinner tonight and they're giving him an award. I'm supposed to go with him, and he'll be arriving at the house any minute now to pick me up. But there's no way I can get back in time to dress and— Excuse me," she told Jed. "I need to find a phone."

Jed watched her slip out of the booth; he would have given several years of his life to be able to erase the last half hour and start over again.

What a terrible time he'd picked to try to convince Cathy that she didn't want *him,* she wanted a man who'd give her a child.

Maybe Bill and Gladys weren't as right about that as they thought, in which case he'd made an even bigger blunder. Maybe what Cathy wanted was someone to share her life with. But that would be even worse.

He couldn't qualify as a candidate.

Still . . . she had told him that she *loved* him and he had flung her words back in her face. She'd never be able to forgive him for that.

He wondered if he could leave the restaurant by the time Cathy got back from making her phone call. But as he was about to stand up, it occurred to him that he didn't have a cent in his pocket. So much for having said that if she didn't want to drive him, he'd call a cab.

Jed shifted position slightly so he could see the telephone at the back of the restaurant. A gray-haired man had been using it, but now he moved away and Cathy took his place.

Cathy's fingers were shaking as she tried to insert coins into the phone. She missed the slot, the coins dropped to the floor and she retrieved them before they rolled out of sight under a radiator.

This time, she managed to insert the coins, and dialed Gladys's number.

Gladys answered on the second ring.

"Oh, Gladys, Gladys," Cathy pleaded, "*please* help me."

"Cathy, what is it?" Gladys asked, alarmed. "You sound terrible."

"I feel terrible. But that isn't—"

"Cathy, what has happened?"

"Everything has just...just crashed between Jed and me, but that's not what I'm calling about. I..."

"What are you talking about? *What* has crashed between you and Jed?"

"I can't get into it right now. Gladys, I really need your help."

"With Jed? Cathy, where are you?"

"Not with Jed, no. With my father."

"The *judge?*"

"Yes."

"What has happened to the judge?"

"Nothing, except that he's due to arrive at my house at any minute, and he'll expect to find me ready to go to the Bar Association dinner with him. There's no way I can get there in time and he shouldn't have to go alone, Gladys. He's getting an award, as well as making a speech. He needs to have a companion with him for the sake of appearance and...morale."

"I doubt your father needs a morale booster, Cathy. But even if he does, what does this have to do with me?"

"Gladys, *please.*. Put on that gorgeous gray satin dress you wore to the Christmas party last year and your pearls, and some of that perfume I gave you that you never use, and go to the dinner with the judge."

"No," Gladys said.

Cathy leaned against the wall, and moaned, "Oh, God. Don't do this to me, Gladys. I thought you liked my father."

"Cathy, your father and I have only met once, and I found him a charming and interesting man. But that doesn't mean that I should get myself gussied up and tell him he's about to have me as a dinner companion."

"You don't have to. I'll call and tell him myself. All you have to do is get dressed as fast as you can and go on over to the house."

"Frankly, Cathy," Gladys said, "if I were to do that I would feel like a fool."

Cathy capitulated. "All right. All *right*.. I'll call Eduardo and tell him to tell the judge to go along to the dinner by himself. It'll be okay."

"Cathy..."

"No, it really is all right, Gladys," Cathy said wearily. "I don't have the right to try to put you into a situation you don't want to be put in, any more than I have the right to put Jed Moriarty into a situation he doesn't want to be put into. Except that Jed is so wrong about almost everything."

"I don't know what you're talking about, dear," Gladys said. "But," she warned, "I'll expect you to tell me later."

She sighed. "Meantime, I'll struggle into the gray satin. I just hope it still fits. I think I've gained at least five pounds in the last year. And you don't have to call Eduardo. I'll call and attempt to explain the situation myself. I guess I'd better also tell Eduardo that you and Jed will be pretty late for dinner."

Gladys didn't wait for an answer. Cathy heard the receiver click at the other end of the line, and she sagged. Her legs felt like rubber; she knew she couldn't hold herself together much longer.

Chapter Fourteen

"I'm sorry we're late, Eduardo," Cathy said.

"*Señorita,* please," Eduardo protested, for once not slipping into Spanish with her. He looked at her anxiously. "I will bring wine and some hors d'oeuvres," Eduardo decided.

"Thank you," Cathy said, "but I don't think I can eat anything. I have a . . . bad headache."

And a worse heartache.

"If you'll excuse me," she said, trying to sound very calm, "I think my best prescription is aspirin, a hot bath and bed."

"*Señorita,*" Eduardo implored, "some dinner first, please. I have prepared the Cuban dish you like so much. *Ropa vieja.*"

Jed looked perplexed. "Old clothes?"

Eduardo laughed. "*Sí.* It is a mixture of meat and spices served on rice and topped with a fried egg. Do not look so distressed, *señor*. The *señorita* will convince you, I think, that it is delicious."

The *señorita* was not about to try to convince him of anything, Jed thought morosely. He had blown it with Cathy.

He turned to her and said gently, "Eduardo's right, Cathy. You do need something to eat before you call it a night. I bet you skipped lunch."

She shrugged. "Yes. But it doesn't matter."

"It does matter. Come in the living room and let Eduardo bring us some wine and snacks. I promise I won't try to keep you after you've had dinner."

Jed looked miserably unhappy, and that made Cathy feel even worse.

He'd said what he'd felt he had to say to her, and now that she'd simmered down somewhat, she realized it had taken courage for him to do that.

"Cathy," Jed said, "if you'd rather, I'm sure Eduardo would take a tray up to you."

"Of course," Eduardo said quickly.

"No, I'll join you for dinner, Jed," she insisted. "But first I'm going to change into something comfortable. Eduardo?"

"Yes, *señorita?*"

"Did the judge and Mrs. Schwartz get off to the dinner on time?"

"Yes, plenty of time." Eduardo's black eyes sparkled. "Mrs. Schwartz, she looked very beautiful. And the judge was most handsome."

"Was he angry, Eduardo?"

"Angry?"

"With me."

"No, the judge was *sorprendido,*" Eduardo said. "Surprised. But he assured Mrs. Schwartz that he was most pleased she was to accompany him. He said that if he had known, he would have sent her an orchid.''

"Hmm," Cathy murmured. "Interesting."

"Most interesting, *señorita*," Eduardo agreed.

Cathy involuntarily pressed her fingers against her temples. Her head was throbbing.

"I'll change and be right back down," she told Jed.

Jed watched her march up the stairs, her back ramrod straight. He was tempted to go after her, then thought better of it. He couldn't hope to make instant peace with Cathy.

He had hurt her feelings, dented her pride. *He* had experienced that kind of rejection, but he doubted if she ever had. Not, certainly, that rejection was what he'd had in mind when he'd vehemently negated her declaration of love.

The crazy thing about it, he thought wryly, was that once again he'd been thinking of *her.* He was going to have to convince her of that, but it wouldn't be easy.

At the best, he had a lot of fence-mending to do with Cathy.

There was a fire blazing on the living-room hearth, and Jed was staring moodily at the leaping flames when Cathy came back downstairs.

A floorboard creaked, and he swung around. Cathy was standing in the doorway, still pale but she looked better. In fact . . . she looked incredibly beautiful.

She was wearing a long velvet robe—Jed thought it was either deep blue or purple—and it looked wonderful on her. It was tied at her waist with a gold cord, and she wore gold slippers. She had pinned her hair up in a knot on the top of her head, and she wasn't wearing any makeup at all.

Jed couldn't hold back. He went to her and put his arms around her.

She stiffened, and he suspected that if she hadn't been afraid she might hurt his hands she would have pushed him away. As it was, she let him draw her closer to him.

As he savored her sweetness, Jed's love for her overflowed. "Sweetheart," he began huskily. "Oh, Cathy, please. I'm so damned sorry. I didn't mean—"

Cathy placed a slim finger against his lips.

"Not now," she said. "I really do have a raging headache and I don't want to get into anything more tonight."

He nodded. "Okay." He glanced ruefully at his bandaged hands. "Eduardo put the wine on the coffee table," he said. "Would you pour, please?"

Cathy filled the wineglasses, and Jed awkwardly cupped his right hand around the glass she handed him. It would be his luck, he thought, if he dropped the glass and it shattered into a thousand pieces. Chances were that it was a valuable antique.

Cathy sat down in an armchair near the fireplace, took a sip of her wine and then set the glass aside.

She was having a hard time dealing with just being around Jed. She didn't think she could handle it if he talked about anything personal. So she forced herself to concentrate on the professional aspects of her relationship with him.

"There's something I forgot to tell you," she began. "Earlier this week, I asked the judge to check on your in-laws."

Startled, Jed asked, "The DiAngelos?"

She nodded.

He frowned. "Why did you do that?"

"I've thought all along that one of them might have it in for you," she reminded him, "and, as it turns out, maybe one of them does. The two older brothers seem to be okay, but the younger one—Mario—has a mixed history. He has an alcohol problem, he's been in and out of mental hospitals. The two older brothers have tried to make a place for him in the family business, but so far it hasn't worked."

"Mario was never interested in the family business. He's always wanted to be a sculptor and I'd say he has some talent . . . but Tony could never see anything like that."

"Was Mario close to his sister?"

Jed nodded reluctantly. "Yes. When Angela died, Mario tried to beat me up."

He stared down into his wineglass, forced to remember things he'd rather forget.

"Why haven't you ever mentioned that?" Cathy asked sharply.

"Because it didn't seem important to me."

"Jed, don't you realize *yet* that someone has such a serious grudge against you they'd maybe just as soon see you dead?"

"Of course I realize that," Jed said impatiently. "But I still don't think it's Mario DiAngelo. Mario has always been mixed-up. I admit he felt a lot of hate for me when Angela died. But he got over it, Cathy. I've told you—there was more grief than hatred involved in the DiAngelos' feelings toward me, except maybe for Tony."

Cathy couldn't hold back the question. "Jed, is it because you loved her so much that you've never really wanted anyone else . . . maybe still don't?"

His voice was hoarse. "Angela?"

"Angela, of course."

"It might be easier if I could say yes to that. I can't. I didn't love Angela. I found out the hard way that I'd never loved Angela. I was infatuated with her, yes...in the beginning. But long before she died I hated her."

Jed added savagely, "Why do you think I despise taking the money I inherited from her? The only reason I took it was because it was my ticket to getting out of the whole miserable situation in Somerville. My Uncle Mike retired a couple of years ago, and now he and his wife live in Florida. But Mike was still involved in the business when Tony died, and by then he and I *really* didn't get along.

"There was no future for me with the company. I should have broken away years earlier, and when I look back I can't believe I didn't. Except that I had first a mother and then a wife I felt I was responsible for—no matter how I felt about the wife.

"It's ironic to think that my first real opportunity came from Angela. I convinced myself I'd be an idiot not to grab it, and I still think that's so. But I intended to pay back every cent to Tony DiAngelo. It's still my intention to pay every cent back to Sam and Benny and Mario.

"Does that answer your question, Cathy?"

Cathy felt too wrung out to reply.

She tried to eat the dish Eduardo had prepared especially for her, but she couldn't. She toyed with the food on her plate, and after a time she excused herself.

She knew that Jed's eyes were following her as she went upstairs, and that he was worried about her. And she wondered what she would do if he came to her room.

It would be very hard to turn him away.

But he didn't come, and after a time Cathy fell into a restless sleep.

At some point, she awakened and heard laughter. She recognized the judge's voice and then Gladys's voice, and it sounded as if they were getting along just fine.

Cathy's lips curved into a bittersweet smile as she drifted back to sleep again.

Rain was splashing against the windowpanes when Cathy woke up the next morning. She looked at her bedside clock. It was almost eight, which meant that she'd overslept and would have to get a move on if she were to get to the office on time.

She still had a dull headache, and her throat hurt. It would have been easy to think she was coming down with something. But she knew what her problem was.

Jed Moriarty.

When she went downstairs, she found the judge at the dining-room table, sipping coffee as he read the *Globe*.

Cathy said immediately, "Dad, I'm sorry about last night. I had every intention of going to the dinner with you."

"Well, I missed you, of course," the judge said gallantly, "but Gladys was a delightful substitute. It was kind of her to stand in for you."

"Did the two of you have a good time?"

"After the dinner, we did. We went over to a lounge Gladys knew about where they have a good combo that plays our kind of music."

"You danced?"

"We danced. She's an excellent dancer, matter of fact."

"So are you."

Cathy poured herself a cup of coffee, and sat down at the table. "Where's Jed?" she asked.

"Getting some rest, I hope," the judge said. "He was watching television when Gladys and I got back last night. After she left, he and I talked for a while. When I decided to go to bed, he said he thought he'd watch some more television. He was restless—I think perhaps his hands were bothering him."

His hands...and a lot of other things, Cathy thought.

She resisted the temptation to go upstairs and check on Jed, reached for a section of the newspaper, then saw that she'd inadvertently chosen the automotive section.

She put it aside. Cars, as cars, were of no particular interest to her, as long as she had one that was a color she liked and ran without giving her any mechanical problems.

Cars and colors. There was something about that combination....

The judge, she saw, was watching her closely. Finally he said, "You look tired, Catherine. I hope you won't have to carry such a heavy workload too much longer. You know, I've been thinking that we might take a cruise at either Thanksgiving or Christmas. Would either time fit in with your schedule?"

"I don't know, Dad," Cathy told him. "Frankly, I'm not making plans right now. There's no telling when Bill will be back in the office, though he's doing extremely well. Until he's back, I can't go on any trips.

When I do get a chance to take some time off, I may just go off somewhere and have myself a quiet nervous breakdown.''

She hadn't meant to say that.

She was thankful that the judge didn't pick her up on it. Instead, he said, ''I have another—this time significant—piece of information about Mario DiAngelo.''

''Oh?''

''He was not in this area last Saturday night when Jed's trailer was destroyed.''

''What are you saying?''

''He was in jail in New Hampshire. He was picked up near Nashua and charged with driving under the influence. He pleaded not guilty, his brothers have retained a lawyer and the case will go to trial. But I doubt Mario will get off. He was drunk, as his blood alcohol level proved, and it's only by the grace of God that a serious accident was avoided. He *could* be facing a manslaughter or even a homicide charge if he hadn't been plain damned lucky. But,'' the judge concluded, ''he is not your arsonist.''

''He still could be,'' Cathy pointed out. ''He could have paid someone to toss that bomb into Jed's trailer. And to vandalize the property. And to torch the two houses last summer.''

''Possibly, but I'm inclined to doubt it. Jed doesn't think Mario is involved, and I tend to agree with him. I think this is someone closer to home, Cathy. Someone who has it against Jed for either a real or imagined wrong.

''Like most people in business, Jed's had a disgruntled employee now and then. He says he's never fired anyone unless he's had to. But the right or wrong of a situation might not make much difference to a psychopath.''

The judge pushed back his chair. ''I'd better get back to the city,'' he announced.

''You drove down?'' Cathy was remembering that Eduardo had the judge's car.

''Yes. I rented a car.''

''Dad, Eduardo has been a great help these past few days, but I think you should have him back in Boston.''

''In good time,'' the judge said easily. ''Right now he's needed here—and he's loving every minute of it.''

Darkness came quickly at the end of October days, and by late afternoon that Friday, Cathy felt an overwhelming need to get some fresh air and exercise.

She glanced out the window and saw that the rain had let up. That was enough to convince her to leave while there was still some daylight left, regardless of the amount of paperwork she should do.

She stopped by her house and put on sweats. There was no sign of either Jed or Eduardo, and she presumed they'd gone somewhere together.

She jogged at an easy pace to a small beach a few blocks away that bordered Hyannis harbor, and sank down on a park bench. The gray water was choppy, the sky above it heavy with dark clouds. Her only companions were two sea gulls, busy foraging for whatever flotsam and jetsam they could find along the water line.

A trawler put out of the harbor, moving toward Nantucket Sound. There was a man on the forward deck wearing a bright yellow slicker, and Cathy was immediately reminded of Jed.

She'd known him for such a short while, and yet there already was so much that would forever remind her of him. Her eyes stung, and when it started to rain again, she felt as if nature were crying with her.

She was drenched by the time she got back to the house, and she cut around to the kitchen door. She turned the handle . . . and came face-to-face with Jed Moriarty.

"Damn," he said explosively, "are you trying to get pneumonia? Look at you! You're soaked."

"That's okay," Cathy told him. "It isn't very cold."

"It's cold enough. Suppose you go take a hot shower and put on something warm, and I'll fix you some tea."

She looked around. "Where's Eduardo?"

"He brought me back from the doctor's, then he went to the mall to do some shopping."

Cathy involuntarily glanced at Jed's hands. The left one was bandaged as heavily as ever, but now he wore only a light gauze dressing on the right.

"Jed, that's terrific," she said.

"Yeah, it helps. Cathy, go get into something dry, will you?"

"Jed," she protested, "I'm fine. Don't worry about me."

"I think I'll always worry about you," Jed said quietly.

Cathy almost melted. Jed looked as desperate and confused as she felt, but despite that, she saw something in his astonishing eyes that staggered her. Maybe Jed would never say the words to her, but the way he was looking at her gave him away.

He loved her.

He *loved* her, dammit.

Her heart started to sing.

"Please," he urged impatiently, "go get those wet things off, will you, then come back down? There's something I have to tell you."

Her hopes soared. "Tell me now. I can wait a few minutes to change."

He scowled, but then said, "Okay. Maybe it's better if I have to make this short. I'll be moving out Monday, Cathy."

Her heart turned to lead.

"So," she said, trying to wrap some pride around her, "you found a place to stay after all."

"Yes. Mrs. Smithson has a furnished apartment over her garage that isn't being used, and she's offered me the use of it for as long as I want."

"I see."

"No," Jed said, "you don't see. This is a business arrangement. Mrs. Smithson isn't doing me any special favors. The rent she could get for the apartment will be taken into consideration in establishing the retainer I'll be paid."

Cathy, heedless of her wet clothes, sat down.

"Genevieve Smithson is paying you a retainer? I thought you said you wouldn't take any money from her."

"I'm not *taking* any money from her. She wants to establish the center for inner-city children I suggested, Cathy. She says the center can be named after Sylvester, and he can be a kind of mascot. But the important thing is that the center will primarily be for kids."

Cathy was sure Jed's enthusiasm was genuine, and under other circumstances it would have been contagious. But right now...

"I'm to work with an architect on the plans. If everything goes as we think it will, I'll get the building contract. We're going to construct buildings for year-round use, although at first the center may operate in summers only. Gradually the program can be expanded."

"It should become a lifetime project," Cathy said dryly.

Jed's eyes narrowed. "I thought you might be happy about it."

"Oh, I am, I am. But aren't you violating your principles just a little bit?"

"I don't think so." Jed paused, then said coldly, "I might remind you that you're the one who told me how great it would be if something worked out for me with Mrs. Smithson."

"Yes, but you certainly disagreed."

Cathy pushed a lock of damp hair from her forehead. "I *am* glad for you, Jed," she said then, and told herself that once she'd recovered from the shock she probably would be. Jed deserved a break in his life, and this could be a very big break. "This should put an end to your financial problems, and—"

Jed cut her off. "Yes," he said, his eyes shades darker than they usually were, "I'll be paid for what I do. But, though it may sound naive to you, I'm not getting into this for money."

He saw her skepticism. "I'm going into this project because I believe in it," he informed her. "I've *been* an inner-city kid. I know the difference an exposure to something like this could make in a kid's life. Over the years we'll be dealing with hundreds of kids...."

When she didn't respond, he said, his voice low, "I'm sorry you think I'm selling out."

"I didn't say that."

"You don't have to. It's written all over your face. It wouldn't take a psychic to figure out that you think I'm taking advantage of an elderly woman because she's taken a liking to me and seems to trust me."

"No," Cathy said slowly, "I don't think you're taking advantage of Genevieve Smithson."

"Try that line again. It didn't sound very convincing the first time."

"Jed, I'm glad for you. But I can't help but wonder what's going to happen to your first dream. Are you going to give up on Cranberry Estates because your plans for the development were lost in the explosion?"

Jed tapped his head. "The plans are in here. Of course I'm not giving up on Cranberry Estates. What gave you that idea?"

"It doesn't seem as if you could do both."

"On the contrary, working on the children's center will give me the opportunity to develop Cranberry Estates the way I want to develop it. I'll be able to buy the kind of materials I want to buy to use in my houses, and I'll be able to hire the kind of craftsmen I want to hire to work for me. No more shortcuts, no more trying to cope with workmen who don't know what they're doing."

He glanced down at his hands. "Even if these don't function too well for a while, I'll be in business again. I'll be able to employ people to do the things I can't do myself, and..."

A comment he had just made sidetracked Cathy.

"Jed," she asked him, "have you had trouble with many of the people who've worked for you?"

"Your father asked me that this morning," Jed said. "I've had run-ins with a couple of men who resented it when I had to fire them. Nothing major, though."

"Would one of them happen to have a green pickup?"

He shook his head. "The cops checked out that angle."

"Maybe you should review any bad situations you've had with people who've worked for you," Cathy said. "What may not have seemed important to you, could be to someone else. People see things differently—"

She broke off, and stared at him.

Jed Moriarty saw things differently than most people did. Colors, anyway.

She drew a deep breath. "Jed," she asked him, "are you sure the pickup truck you've been seeing is green?"

"Sure," he said. "It's about the same color as my pickup...except that it's not as vivid a shade and anyway it's so filthy..."

"Your pickup isn't green, Jed. It's red, like that sweater you've been wearing. Bright, fire-engine red."

Cathy felt like wringing her hands and tearing her hair out.

"*Why* didn't I think about that before now?" She was furious with herself. "I seldom remember that you're color-blind, especially since you stopped wearing those ghastly combinations."

"I'm the one who should have thought of it," Jed said grimly. "But I'm so accustomed to seeing things *my* way. Most of the time I never really know if I'm right or wrong, but that doesn't usually bother me. I'm used to it.''

Cathy was on her way to the phone. "I'll call the Cedarville police first," she said. "Then I'll get Don Crandon. He probably won't be in his office this late but he'll check for messages."

As she looked up the number of the Cedarville police, she reproached herself audibly. "If I had used half a brain I would have questioned your description of the pickup. Then the explosion would never have happened. Your hands..."

Cathy swallowed hard. "Your hands," she said unsteadily, "would never have been burned."

God, how she'd failed him, she thought, miserable. Just looking at the bandages on his hands made her feel sick.

Jed stopped her before she could dial. "Knock it off," he commanded roughly.

Cathy's eyes widened as she saw his expression. He was incensed.

"You're a very smart lady," he gritted, "but you're neither all-seeing nor all-powerful. No one is. As I said, *I'm* the one who shouldn't have been so damned positive about giving anyone a color description. That wasn't your fault."

The anger faded from Jed's face, and he said more gently, "You've done everything for me anyone possibly could do. But if you fall into the mind-set I see coming on, you're going to be trapped in guilt... and pity. If that happens, then there really never *can* be anything between the two of us, Cathy. Anyway," Jed reminded her, "no one's found him yet. And maybe no one ever will."

* * *

But the police did find him.

His name was Manuel Berger and he lived in a tumbledown shack deep in the woods, about three or four miles from Cranberry Estates.

Jed had to admit that he'd forgotten Berger existed. Berger wasn't someone people tended to remember. He was a small, wiry, nondescript man, and the most significant thing about him was that he had a history of paranoia.

When Jed saw him—through a one-way window in a police lineup in Cedarville—he remembered that Berger was one of the first workmen he'd hired, and he'd lasted less than two weeks.

"He showed up drunk most of the time," Jed recalled. "I couldn't trust him to follow through on even a small job."

He had given Berger an extra week's pay when he let him go, and the man had accepted it and left without protest.

"I never gave him a second thought," Jed admitted.

Berger had not owned a pickup truck then. He'd driven a rusty old Ford sedan that he'd totaled one winter night. Then he had acquired the pickup and, as the police had suspected, he drove it primarily along back roads at night, as he plotted ways to get even with Jed Moriarty.

By Sunday night, Berger was in jail. There were so many charges against him that there was virtually no chance of his going free.

"But it's doubtful he'll ever go to prison," Jed reported to Cathy, after Eduardo had driven him back from a trip to the Cedarville police station. "The cops figure he'll be found not guilty by reason of insanity, and he'll probably spend the rest of his life in a mental institution.''

Jed had insisted that he go to Cedarville alone this time, and Cathy had yielded to his wish.

He no longer needed her services as an attorney, anyway, she thought, and an odd kind of neutrality had developed between the two of them.

After Jed finished telling her about Berger on Sunday night, they didn't seem to have much to say to each other.

He was using his right hand pretty well, Cathy noticed, but there wasn't much doubt that his left one would be crippled, at least to some extent.

She was to blame for that, and she could see no way that she could ever convince herself otherwise.

Chapter Fifteen

Cathy didn't want to say goodbye to Jed.

She reminded herself that he wasn't going to the moon. Genevieve Smithson lived in nearby Osterville. But...once he moved out, nothing would be the same.

Naturally, they'd continue to see each other. They had unfinished business between them, for one thing. The only records Jed had left that dealt with Cranberry Estates were in her office. She'd have to decide whether to keep them for a while, give them back to him or turn them over to Bill Grant. It depended on which of them was going to rectify his credit situation and make arrangements for paybacks—something that shouldn't be difficult to do now that he was employed by Mrs. Smithson.

Regardless, she and Jed would stay in touch. But after today it just wouldn't be the same.

Cathy tried to accept that as she stood looking out her bedroom window early Monday morning. But she didn't do very well. She kept thinking of how empty her house was going to be without Jed.

In such a short time, he had filled both her home and her heart. They belonged together, dammit, she thought, blinking back tears as she saw the first streaks of daylight in the east. They were both just too strong-willed, proud and independent to admit it.

Of course there were obstacles. She knew that Jed had hang-ups about the differences in their background and upbringing; every now and then he showed that. She'd had a few hang-ups about him, and she still smarted when she thought of the way he'd denied her sudden declaration of love.

No one could go back, Cathy told herself. She and Jed both needed to start *now* and go forward, but she didn't think she had the strength left to convince Jed of that. Right now, she was holding herself together with some pretty fragile glue.

She suddenly knew that there was no way she could face Jed this morning.

She simply had to get out of here.

Cathy dressed for work, even though it was only six o'clock, and slipped down the stairs in her stocking feet. Even Eduardo wasn't up yet. She stole across the backyard to the garage, then tried to keep noise to a minimum as she eased her car out onto the driveway.

Jed, who had been awake more than he'd been asleep, heard the car motor and made tracks to the window just in time to see Cathy turn into the street.

He glanced at the sky. The sun was barely up, and she was taking off. Another glance, this time at the clock on the dresser, verified that it was just past six.

Where the hell was Cathy going at this hour of the morning?

Jed flung the window open and stuck out his head, and bellowed Cathy's name. But her car windows were closed, and she was too far away, anyhow. There was no way she could have heard him.

He slumped down on the edge of the bed and tried to follow a lifetime habit of running his fingers through his hair when he was agitated.

The bandages on his hands foiled that, and he stared at them resentfully. This was no time to be shackled . . . by anything.

Jed groaned, struggled into some jeans and a sweater, and went downstairs. Though Eduardo wasn't around yet, he'd set up the coffeemaker.

Jed pushed the button, and within seconds the scent of coffee began to filter through the kitchen. It was an aroma that had a lot of nostalgia connected with it. Fresh, hot coffee, Jed thought, was something to be shared.

So were a lot of other things.

It took a loud rap on the back door to shake him out of a mounting depression. Hope flared as he thought maybe Cathy had come back. But it wasn't Cathy standing at the kitchen door, it was Gladys.

She looked as if she were still half-asleep as she demanded, "What's going on here?" She moved into the kitchen. "Why was Cathy taking off like a bat out of hell with the sun hardly up?"

That was a slight exaggeration, but Gladys could be forgiven, Jed thought. He more than shared her concern about Cathy.

Gladys eyed him narrowly. "Did the two of you have a fight?"

"Not exactly," he hedged.

"What's 'not exactly' supposed to mean? People either have a fight or they don't."

Gladys filled two mugs with coffee, and pushed one across the counter to Jed. She was eyeing him, Jed thought, as if he'd committed a crime.

"Would you mind trying to tell me what's going through your head, Moriarty?" she asked him, sounding like a school principal who'd been called in to deal with an especially recalcitrant pupil. "Why are you moving out of here into an apartment over Genevieve Smithson's garage, for one thing? Why don't you stick around and persuade Cathy that the two of you should get married and have a couple of kids before it's too late?"

Jed's jaw dropped. "Are you out of your mind?"

"No," Gladys said, "but I'm wondering if maybe you're out of yours. All anyone has to do is look at the two of you, and it would take an idiot not to realize there's a lot going on. Even Howard said so."

"Who?"

"The judge," Gladys said.

"The *judge?*"

"Jed, are you having a problem with your hearing?"

Gladys took another peek at him and began to relent a little. There were dark smudges under his eyes; he looked tired and vulnerable. It was a long time since she'd felt a surge of maternal instinct but one began to brew now.

She asked gently, "You do love her, don't you?"

Jed nearly choked. Then he heaved a deep breath and admitted, "Yeah, I love her. I love her so damned much I don't know whether I'm coming or going."

"Then why are you doing this?"

"I'm not doing anything. I mean, I'm only doing what I have to do." Jed shrugged. "You're a reasonable person, Gladys. Just think about Cathy and think about me and . . . what do you see?"

"A pretty striking couple," Gladys Schwartz told him.

Cathy didn't know where she was going. She just knew that she was damned if she'd get to the office early, which meant that she had nearly three hours to kill.

She followed the highway to the west end of the Cape, then turned onto a side road that led to the Cape Cod Canal. There were a few fishermen trying their luck, and one of them struck a payload. She watched as he hauled in a magnificent striper.

She followed the old King's Highway down the Cape, and stopped at a little restaurant where she drank some coffee and, for the most part, crumbled a cranberry muffin.

At eight-thirty, she gave up and went to work.

Gladys arrived at the office five minutes later than Cathy and made straight for Cathy's private sanctum.

"What got into you?" she asked. "You woke both Jed and me up, and he was as worried as I was."

"There was no reason for either of you to worry, Gladys. I just wanted to get out of the house for a while."

"Aren't you saying that you wanted to walk out on Jed?"

Cathy stiffened. "I think you're putting that backward. Jed's walking out on me."

"No, boss lady," Gladys contradicted. "Jed is not walking out on you. He's moving into his own apartment for the time being, which will be easier for him while he works on Genevieve Smithson's project. Remember, he still can't drive."

"I haven't forgotten, Gladys."

"Mrs. Smithson has a car and chauffeur she can put at his disposal when he needs transportation, until he's able to drive again himself."

"Damn it, he had Eduardo," Cathy blurted.

"One of these days Eduardo will be going back to Cambridge, Cathy."

Gladys sat down, and there was a rather strange look on her face that puzzled Cathy.

"Your father has invited me to come up to Cambridge next weekend," she said, "and I was wondering how you might feel about that?"

"I think the two of you have already wasted the better part of two years because of me."

"What?"

"Gladys, I can't begin to tell you how much I've wished that there were someone other than me, and maybe Eduardo, who really counted in the judge's life. But I knew that whoever it might be would have to be a very special person."

Cathy frowned. "Now what irks me is that I didn't see the tree for the forest. The two of you are so right for each other."

Gladys said quietly, "You and Jed are right for each other, too, Cathy." Hastily she added, "Anyway, don't you think you're rushing things where the judge and I are concerned? We've only seen each other a couple of times."

"How long does it take?" Cathy asked, and knew the answer.

She'd come close to love at first sight with Jed Moriarty. She could see that now.

By lunchtime, she was so restless it was all she could do to sit still, and she kept tapping her gold pen against the desk blotter.

She finally had to escape, and she took off, warning Gladys that she might be a while.

She drove across to the old King's Highway again, which had more than its share of antique shops, parked and began to browse through some. She had in mind to find, or try to find, a candelabra for her dining-room sideboard. She'd wanted one for a long time, and maybe, she thought, this might be the time to give herself a present. Self-indulgence was, perhaps, better than nothing at all.

She didn't see anything she liked in the first couple of shops. But in the third one, something far removed from a candelabra caught her eye.

Nestled in a leather box lined with thick blue plush almost the color of Jed's eyes lay a shiny brass telescope.

Cathy glanced at the price tag, and winced.

Three thousand dollars?

The proprietor approached and said, "That's quite a beauty. An antique refractor, French in origin and signed by the maker. You're interested in astronomy?"

"I was thinking about a gift for a friend."

The man smiled. "An expensive gift, I admit. But you couldn't go wrong with this. It's a treasure. My guarantee goes with it."

A minute later, Cathy reached into her handbag for her checkbook. She couldn't believe she was doing this; it was the first time in her life she had ever yielded to such an impulse. Maybe it was because the plush lining so nearly matched the color of Jed's eyes, she thought, as she carried the long case out to her car. But she wanted this for him, even though she had absolutely no idea of how she was going to give it to him without him giving it right back to her.

She put the case in the car trunk, and all afternoon at work she felt as though she were harboring a guilty secret. A couple of times she was tempted to tell Gladys what she had done, but she couldn't bring herself to confess that she'd been so impetuous.

It was late afternoon when Gladys appeared, and asked, "Ready for tonight?"

"What's happening tonight?"

"This is Halloween. Did you forget?"

Yes, she'd forgotten, Cathy thought ruefully. And she had intended to decorate her house for Halloween with cotton cobwebs and plastic skeletons and pumpkin lanterns with candles in them. She had even thought about buying herself a witch's costume so she could dress up and have fun pretending to scare the trick-or-treaters when they rang her doorbell.

She settled for stopping by a supermarket and loading up on lollipops and small chocolate bars.

It was dark by the time she pulled into her driveway. Worse than that, her house was dark, too, and there were no lights in Gladys's apartment.

It wasn't surprising that Gladys was out, though she'd given the impression she'd be home tonight to receive small guests.

But where was Eduardo? The judge's car was neither in the garage nor in the driveway. Also, the lights that lined the path up to the house were out, and so was the light over the front door.

Irritated, Cathy struggled up the walk with her bags of treats and the telescope in its case. She had to fumble for her key, and it was no mean feat to insert it into the lock. Then she pushed the door open, stepped into her house and froze as a deep, sepulchral voice warned, "Don't move!"

She'd wondered, sometimes, what she would do if she ever walked into her house and found an intruder there. Scream, maybe? If she screamed right now, no one would hear her.

Her only viable weapons were the bags of candies, and the telescope. She was poised to take action and swing, when she realized she didn't even know where her potential assailant *was*. It was darker than pitch in the room, and she couldn't see a thing.

That was enough to start fear's icy fingers snaking along her spine.

The sepulchral voice demanded, "Which is it to be? A trick or a treat?"

Cathy felt a large, human presence come closer, and a familiar scent wafted toward her—male, spicy and unforgettable.

"Jed," she bellowed, "damn you!"

"Quiet, woman," Jed Moriarty commanded. He flicked a switch, and the overhead living-room lights blazed in Cathy's face.

She was so startled, she screamed. But before she could make a move, Jed commanded, "Close your eyes."

Cathy's eyes were glued to his face. "Why?" she demanded.

"Just do it, will you?" he growled. "For once in your life just do something someone asks you to do without stopping to create a legal brief about it."

She shut her eyes.

"Now," Jed instructed her, "put down all that stuff you're carrying, then with your eyes still closed, move around in a circle to the right.... Next, walk forward five steps.... Okay, now turn to the left and walk back three steps, then turn to the left again...."

"What is this?" Cathy demanded.

"You can look now."

Cathy opened her eyes and saw the exquisite baby grand piano in the corner. The mellow wood was polished to a gleaming finish. The bench was positioned as if at any second someone would sit down and begin to play....

She was so staggered, she couldn't speak.

She moved toward the piano as if she were in a trance, and tentatively touched a key. Then she turned to Jed, still speechless, and was bewildered by his expression.

She would have thought he'd be smiling. Instead, he was watching her apprehensively, his eyes wary.

"I hope you like it." His voice was very low.

"*Like* it?" How could she possibly tell him how she felt? "Jed, you'll never know how much I've wanted a piano. But...it just wasn't something I would get for myself."

"I know you already have a piano at your father's place in Cambridge, Cathy."

"Yes," she admitted, "and I'm sure the judge wouldn't have objected to my bringing it to the Cape. But...I'm not sure I can explain this. My feelings about the piano in Cambridge are somehow tangled up with my giving up music in favor of the law, mostly to please my father.

"Maybe I've resented that more than I've admitted, even to myself," she added thoughtfully. "And I shouldn't. Either my talent wasn't great enough for me to become a concert pianist or my motivation wasn't strong enough. Or nothing would have stopped me."

There was still that wary expression in Jed's eyes. "Are you saying that if someone wants something enough, nothing will stop them?"

"Yes. I'm beginning to believe that."

She lightly ran a scale with her right hand, then flipped thumb and little finger through a series of octaves, and said in surprise, "It's in perfect tune."

"We had it tuned this afternoon."

"We?"

"The piano belonged to Genevieve Smithson," Jed said, "but it's never been used much. Her husband bought it for her a long time ago, and she intended to take lessons, but she never did. She says she hates it when something that should be used isn't. So when I asked her if I could buy it from her, she agreed. She helped me get a tuner, and some men to move it over here. Maybe this isn't just where you want it, but..."

Jed added, almost defiantly, "Mrs. Smithson didn't give the piano to me, Cathy. I'm buying it from her. We've worked out a payment schedule."

Cathy smiled. "You don't have to sound so belligerent," she said softly. "I believe you."

She rubbed her fingers over the tops of the black keys. "One of these days, before long, I'll play for you," she promised. "But not now. First I need to do some practicing in private. The first time I play for you I want it to be good."

She groped for words. "Oh, Jed, Jed, this is a very big gift. It shows me you can see straight into my heart."

Jed wondered if she could see into his heart; and, if so, what she'd think about what she saw there. His love for her was brimming over, but he still didn't know how to handle it.

Cathy had so totally altered the course of his life. It was because of her that he'd met Genevieve Smithson, and that in itself was opening up a whole new world. It was she who had realized that he'd inadvertently been giving the police the wrong information, so now Manuel Berger would never set fire to anything else again.

Last night, he'd been appalled by her conviction that she was to blame for what had happened to his hands. God, but for her realizing what she had, he would have gone back to Cedarville once he had the insurance money and tried again, and the next time he might not have been so lucky.

He had to convince her that she was not guilty of anything, except causing him to fall in love with her. And she damned well stood convicted of *that*.

His hands would heal, Jed thought. But he wasn't at all sure his heart would. He had to find a way to show Cathy how much she meant to him. Even then, he wasn't sure he'd ever be right for her....

While Jed tried to find the first words to say, the doorbell pealed.

Cathy said, "Eduardo will get it." Then, remembering, she asked Jed, "Where *is* Eduardo?"

"Er...I asked him to skip out for a couple of hours," Jed admitted.

"And Gladys?"

"She's up in her place. I asked her to keep her lights off till you got into the house, and she said she was going to keep them off anyway to create a little atmosphere for the kids."

The doorbell rang again, and Jed said, "Speaking of kids..."

Cathy grabbed the bags of candies, and said, "Douse the lights, Jed."

"What?"

"When I open the door, you do that voice of yours, and I'll dole out the treats."

The small spaceman, fairy princess and hideous monster who stood on Cathy's front step were carrying flashlights that revealed puzzled little faces as they peered into the darkened house.

Then Jed intoned, "Trick or treat?" in a voice that sounded as though it came from the bottom of a vampire's cage, and the children squealed with delight as Cathy tossed candies into their orange paper sacks.

Ghosts and witches and mermaids and knights and ballerinas and hobos and a variety of hobgoblins followed, to be frightened by Jed and treated by Cathy.

Cathy finally dispensed the last candy and closed the door, then leaned against it and smiled happily. She couldn't remember when she'd had so much fun.

Then she saw that Jed was staring at something. With the bags of treats gone, the telescope was standing all by itself on the living-room floor.

Jed's face was wiped clean of all expression as he said, "I guess I don't have to ask you what that is."

Cathy brushed past him and picked up the case, then set it down on the coffee table. "I intended to present it a bit more effectively," she said. She opened the case as she spoke. The telescope gleamed against the rich blue background.

"You shouldn't have gotten it," Jed said.

"Jed, please, it's a present."

He shook his head. "I couldn't possibly take that kind of present from you."

She'd warned herself that she might expect something like this. Even so...

"You want a telescope as much as I want a piano," she said unsteadily.

"I can't deny that. But this..."

His voice was ragged. "God, Cathy, no one in my entire life has ever given me anything like this. I've never *had* anything like this. And I don't want it from you."

He tried to explain. "It...it symbolizes everything that stands between us, can't you see that? Maybe someday I'll be able to, but right now I can't imagine just going out and...and buying something like this."

Cathy chose her words carefully. "The best things can't be bought, Jed. Like bringing the moon and the planets and the stars closer. But this can do that. And...that's something I want to share with you. I want you to share my music, and I want to share your stars. And . . ."

He waited.

Cathy's laugh was shaky. "I'm damned if I'm going to propose to you, Moriarty."

Jed saw a tear trickle down her cheek, and that did it. He held his arms out to her and urged, "Come here."

His eyes looked like dark sapphires, and a mix of emotions played across his face. He tugged Cathy close, and warned, "Don't look at me, or I won't have the guts to say what I need to say."

Jed took a deep breath. "I love you, Catherine Merrill. I love you, and I want to marry you, and I want us to have children, and I want to live with you and keep right on loving you and grow old with you. . . ."

Cathy tilted back her head. "Moriarty," she asked, "are we finally agreeing about something?"

Jed's eyes glistened as he brushed her forehead with his lips, then touched her soft bronze hair with his five working fingers. He traced her eyebrows and her nose and her chin, and it was wonderful to touch her again.

He fumbled for the zipper on the back of her dress, and said huskily, "Maybe you'd better help. I'm still awkward as hell."

"Maybe we'd better go upstairs," Cathy said, "unless we want Eduardo to walk in on us."

Then her gaze fell on an object sharing the coffee table with Jed's telescope and she went over and picked up the little Aladdin's lamp.

"Thanks for finding Mr. Perfect for me," she whispered softly.

Jed asked, "What was that about?" as they started up the stairs together.

Cathy smiled. "I was talking to my genie," she told him.

* * * * *

VOWS
A series celebrating marriage
by Sherryl Woods

To Love, Honor and Cherish—these were the words that three
generations of Halloran men promised their women they'd live
by. But these vows made in love are each challenged by the
tests of time....

In October—Jason Halloran meets his match in *Love #769;*

In November—Kevin Halloran rediscovers love—with his
wife—in *Honor #775;*

In December—Brandon Halloran rekindles an old flame in
Cherish #781.

These three stirring tales are coming down the aisle toward
you—only from Silhouette Special Edition!

SESW-1